BRING HOLLY HOME
BOOK ONE IN THE REMEMBER ME SERIES

AMANDA RADLEY

SIGN UP TO WIN

Firstly, thank you for purchasing *Bring Holly Home* I really appreciate your support and hope you enjoy the book!

Head over to my website and sign up to my mailing list to be kept up to date with all my latest releases, promotions, and giveaways.

www.amandaradley.com

BRING HOLLY HOME

CHAPTER ONE

Louise took a deep breath and quickly started to recite the schedule to her boss.

"So, as you know, the gala is tonight. The table plan is in your room for final approval as you requested. Your car arrives tomorrow at ten o'clock to take you to Charles de Gaulle. I'll be checking out of the hotel earlier to get the Guerlain samples that you requested for your sister, so I'll meet you at the airport at quarter to eleven."

Louise knew this was an exercise in futility. Her boss knew the schedule back to front, and yet she felt the urgent need to fill the awkward silence that permeated the back of the limousine. She subtly turned her wrist in her lap to look at her watch.

"Hm," Victoria murmured.

Louise looked up to see if her boss would say anything else.

Victoria continued to look over the top of her glasses at the passing Parisian scenery.

Louise debated if she should say something else. Maybe

give another rundown on the first-class menu on offer onboard the flight from Paris to New York. Maybe attempt to get a tiny amount of kudos for having changed the red meat option from lamb for the entire cabin, simply because Victoria couldn't abide the smell of lamb.

Not that Victoria would ever acknowledge any of the backbreaking, soul-destroying work that Louise did on a daily basis for the impossible-to-please woman. But she lived in hope that a nugget of gratitude would work its way into Victoria's conscience.

Maybe enough to promote her from her role of assistant. Being an assistant to Victoria Hastings was certainly prestigious. Sadly, it didn't pay the therapy bills that Louise would need if she managed to survive the role.

Louise's mobile phone rang, and she answered immediately. "Yes?"

It was that awful French man from the gazette again. Blathering on about something or other and making little sense.

"Look, I've told you before, Victoria will not be doing any interviews. If you wanted to speak to her then you should have called *before* she arrived in Paris for Fashion Week. Do you have any idea how busy she is? Of course you don't."

The man continued talking hurriedly. Louise just shook her head, not even bothering to listen to what he was saying. She couldn't believe the audacity of the man. Thinking that Victoria Hastings of all people would be able to drop everything and speak to some nobody. Did he have any idea who she was?

"Absolutely not, and don't call this number again!"

Louise huffed, hung up the phone, and tossed it into her bag.

"Damn French," she mumbled under her breath.

"Problem?"

Louise looked up and realised that Victoria had turned to glance at her. Louise took pride in her appearance, checking her reflection at least every twenty minutes to ensure she was looking her best. But the second Victoria looked at her, she felt certain that she must appear a wreck.

Victoria was the kind of woman who always looked perfect. She must have had a long conversation with Mother Nature in which she put her foot down and insisted she wasn't going to age another minute. And so, forty-seven-year-old Victoria Hastings looked like a perfectly turned-out woman in her mid-thirties. Not a hair was out of place in her fashionable blonde bob. Her makeup was light but always on point, just enough to rouge her cheeks, plump her lips, and accentuate her steely green eyes. Nothing less could be expected of the editor of one of the world's leading fashion magazines.

Louise realised that she had been silent for too long. Her panic at potentially not looking her best under Victoria's frosty glare had thrown her.

"Um. No, no problem, Victoria. Just a journalist, some awful little French man. You know what journalists are like. I don't even know why I bother sending out press guidelines. He has been calling me here and Claudia back in New York every single day... I... He..." Louise swallowed nervously.

She'd said too much, she'd bothered Victoria with details that were of no interest to her.

Victoria simply stared at her in silence. Slowly, she rolled her eyes. Louise was sure that Victoria was internally questioning the incompetence she was surrounded by. She usually did. Now it was just a matter of whether Victoria would deliver a softly spoken, but scathing, remark, or if she would ignore her. Louise held her breath while she waited for judgement to be passed.

After a few more frosty seconds, Victoria turned and looked out of the car window again. The conversation was over.

Louise released the breath she had been holding. Silently.

Paris Fashion Week was everything she'd hoped it would be. The shows, the designers, the clothes, the city. But now it was drawing to a close. Three months of doing nothing but planning Victoria's schedule had paid off. It had been a success. Not that anyone would know it from Victoria's expression.

From the moment they had landed in Paris, her boss has been quiet and detached. More so than usual. At the best of times, no one would ever accuse Victoria of being friendly or talkative. In fact, Victoria was famously known for destroying careers with a simple look.

But the last few days had been worse than usual.

Louise reminded herself that there was just one more night between her and her comfy bed back home in New York. And the next morning she would be getting to the airport bright and early and thankfully not travelling with Victoria.

CHAPTER TWO

THE ELEVATOR DOORS SLID OPEN, and Victoria put on her oversized Gucci sunglasses. She walked through the lobby of the Shangri-La Hotel, her heels tapping loudly on the marble flooring.

She could sense the receptionists discreetly looking at her as she walked past them. She imagined that they were breathing a sigh of relief at her departure.

The doorman, dressed in a top hat and a knee-length, forest green overcoat, opened the door as she approached. She breezed through and down the steps.

She let out an audible sigh at the fact that her limousine wasn't in place. She looked up with annoyance to see that the vehicle was on its way down the hotel's driveway, just passing through the wrought iron gates.

"Apologies, Ms Hastings."

She turned to see the manager of the hotel rushing down the steps. He waved his arms frantically to hurry the black limousine up. The moment it came to a stop in front of the steps, he opened the back door and gestured into the car.

"Thank you for your stay. I do hope you found everything to your liking?"

Victoria hummed half-heartedly. While the Shangri-La was slightly above average in some respects, there had been some issues. For starters, the intolerable noise of the fan in her room and the maintenance imbecile who said he couldn't even hear the noise when she had been positively deafened by it.

She passed the grovelling man and got in the back of the limo.

"We do hope to see you again next year," the man continued, holding the door open and looking at her with a pleading expression.

Victoria felt that it was very unlikely that she'd ever come back should he continue to delay her. She wanted to get to the airport and take a few private moments to call her children to see how they were doing. She travelled a lot, but she never stopped missing them.

She was about to instruct the driver to go, regardless of the position of the passenger door, when she noticed the manager looking up the driveway with a frown. She could hear some kind of commotion from behind the car.

"*Excusez-moi,* Madame Hastings!"

She glanced out of the back window. A scruffy-looking man was running towards the car. It looked like he had run through the gates as they were being closed. He held up a piece of paper and was running determinedly towards her. Two doormen and a security guard were chasing after him.

She turned around and called out to the driver in a bored tone, "Go."

The hotel manager closed the passenger door and the car slowly started to edge forward, the sharp turn of the driveway making a quicker departure impossible.

She heard shouts behind the car and rolled her eyes. It seemed nothing was going to go right during this trip.

There was a thump on the window. The scruffy man stood beside the car, holding up a Polaroid photograph. Victoria felt her mouth fall open in shock at the image.

It was Holly Carter. Her former assistant. The one who had abandoned her without a word exactly one year ago. However, there were vast differences between the Holly she had known and the woman in the photograph.

In contrast to Holly's long locks, the photograph showed a woman with short hair. Victoria's artistic sensibilities balked at the change. Long hair was finally back in fashion and the girl had chopped all of hers off. Not that Holly was ever one to toe the line when it came to fashion trends.

But the real shock was the unresponsiveness in her eyes. They no longer sparkled, there was a dullness to them that Victoria had never seen before. And Holly's already pale skin seemed paler, almost sickly in appearance. The forced smile failed to distract from the fact that she looked quite frightened.

As quickly as the photograph had been slapped onto the glass, it was pulled away. Each doorman grabbed one of the scruffy man's arms and dragged him away from the car.

"Wait," she instructed the driver.

Victoria felt the brakes being applied, and the car came

to a jolting stop. She opened the door and stepped out of the car.

The man was now on the tarmac, the two burly doormen on top of him, trying to hold him down. He looked up at her.

"You know her?" he asked, his voice thick with a French accent.

"Let him go," she commanded in a soft tone.

The doormen looked in confusion at the manager who was standing helplessly by. He quickly waved his hands up to indicate that they should let him go.

Slowly, the man climbed to his feet. He clutched the photo in his hand and looked at Victoria expectantly.

She looked him up and down. She had no idea who he was or what he wanted, but he seemed to know Holly. And that was enough to grant him a few moments of her time. Even if she was running late.

She pointed to the car.

"Get in," she instructed.

CHAPTER THREE

THE LIMOUSINE PULLED AWAY from the hotel for the second time. Victoria sat very still in her seat. She watched as the scruffy little French man attempted to make himself less of a mess by adjusting the hem of his appallingly coloured T-shirt.

"*Merci*," he said through panted breaths.

Victoria stared at him, wondering what to make of him.

"*Qui êtes-vous?*" she asked.

"My name is Samuel Durand," he replied in thickly accented English. "I cannot believe that I saw you on the television beside Clémence and now I am talking to you."

"Clémence?" Victoria asked. She had no idea who or what he was referring to and was becoming a little uncomfortable with the situation.

"Clémence Dubois," Samuel answered. He held up the photo of Holly Carter.

"That is *not* Clémence Dubois," Victoria said coldly.

He looked at the photo. "To us, she is. That's the name

that was given to her. She was a, what do you say? A Jane Doe?"

Victoria stared at Samuel in confusion.

"Jane Doe," he repeated. "For someone with no name?"

She reached out her hand and took the photograph from his. She lowered it into her lap delicately and stared down at the image, afraid of the terrible reality it posed. This woman was both Holly and a stranger all at once. The confusion and the warring emotions knotted her stomach.

"Was?" she asked. "You said, 'She was.'" A shudder struck her.

"Is, *is*," he corrected quickly.

Victoria sagged against the leather of the car seat in relief. She looked down at the photo, scarcely believing what she was seeing.

"I'm a freelance journalist," Samuel explained. "My friend works at the hospital and told me a story of an American with no memory. They called her Clémence. I went to interview her. She was brought to the hospital just under a year ago, it was six months later when I met her. She was in an accident. Her head…"

Victoria looked up to see Samuel touching the palm of his hand to the back of his head. She understood that his language skills were preventing him from explaining the details. She nodded for him to continue.

"The authorities tried to locate her family. The American embassy was involved, but nothing happened. I told Clémence that I would try to help her, but I could find nothing." He gestured to Victoria. "And then, when I had almost given up, I saw you on the news. Some old footage showed Clémence with you—"

"Holly," Victoria interrupted in a whisper. "Her name is Holly."

"Holly." He wrapped his mouth around the new name and smiled. "Holly?"

"Holly Carter."

"Holly Carter," he repeated. "Do you wish to see her now?"

Victoria felt icy cold shock pour down the back of her starched collar. It was incomprehensible that Holly was somehow still in France, a year after she had abandoned her job and walked away.

"We can go to the hospital now? I know her doctor will be very pleased to see you," Samuel pressed.

"S-she…" Victoria stuttered uncharacteristically. "She's still in the hospital, now?"

"*Oui.*" Samuel nodded.

Victoria felt her mouth drop open. Her gaze fell back to the photo. She distantly heard Samuel call up to the driver and provide him with the hospital's address.

"Madame Hastings?" The driver requested her approval for the change of destination.

"*Oui,*" she said softly. She didn't look up from the photo.

She felt the long vehicle lurch gently as it performed a U-turn. Her stomach did the same. The anger she had been holding onto crumbled. Guilt washed over her like a tidal wave, and she struggled to breath.

When Holly had vanished twelve months before, Victoria had felt betrayal that quickly turned to fury. The disappearing act of her second assistant had left her under-staffed and embarrassed. While she wasn't one to listen to gossip, she could hear the whispers during the catwalks and galas. She'd arrived with an attentive second assistant and left alone and humiliated.

Of course, she'd had assistants walk out on her before. She wasn't exactly an easy person to work for. Countless names and faces blurred into one large disappointment, the people who couldn't take the pressure, not ready for the greatness they could aspire to if they managed to survive a paltry two years of service.

Some handed in a letter of resignation, some ran crying from the building. Occasionally some vanished without a trace, only for a request for a reference to appear from a new prospective employer a few weeks later.

Holly's disappearing act had taken Victoria by surprise. The girl had always been diligent and professional. Until the moment she vanished without a trace. Victoria had assumed that she'd pushed Holly too far during the previous year's Fashion Week, suspected that the girl had finally snapped and left.

As the weeks and months passed, she was surprised to not hear anything. Not even a request for a reference. She supposed the girl had wisely set herself up in another state, or another country, to avoid Victoria's wrath.

But Victoria prided herself on her professional ethics. Had a letter requesting a reference arrived on her desk, she would have provided a glowing recommendation. Holly Carter may have left her in the middle of the most important event and in the most crucial week in the fashion calendar, but she was still the best assistant that Victoria had ever had. Not that Holly knew that, of course. She'd never actually said the words. Much less hinted at them.

Now it was clear why no one had heard from Holly in the twelve months that had passed. Something terrible had happened. Maybe even the very night when Victoria was packing her own suitcase to fly back to New York, cursing Holly's very existence as she did.

A head injury. Memory loss. Stuck in a hospital in a foreign country.

She quickly put the photograph on the seat between herself and Samuel. Turning, she looked out of the window and attempted to calm her breathing. She needed to compose herself, she wasn't about to lose control in front of some dishevelled journalist.

She could hear Samuel speaking on his mobile phone. Her French was not entirely fluent and his animated speech was difficult to keep up with, but she could ascertain that he was speaking with someone at the hospital. When he referred to Victoria as Holly's friend, she bit back a laugh.

The truth was, she was most likely the very last person in the world Holly would want to see.

CHAPTER FOUR

THE LIMOUSINE PULLED up outside the hospital. Victoria looked up at the imposing old building and took a deep, steadying breath.

Samuel exited the car and jogged around to open Victoria's door for her. He was clearly in a hurry to fulfil his wish to see the two women immediately reacquainted. But Victoria, who had never dawdled in her life, suddenly felt like her muscles were coated in syrup.

With a deep breath, she pulled herself out of the car and wondered again what she was getting herself into. She debated getting back into the car and instructing the driver to take her to the airport. Louise could deal with this. Holly was just an assistant, an assistant who had left her.

Before she could react, the main door to the building opened and a woman hurried towards Samuel. She was young and wore a dark blue nurses' uniform. She pulled Samuel into a hug, and the two swayed back and forth with elation.

A second woman exited the hospital. She was older and

wore a light grey suit topped with a crisp, white medical coat. Her greying hair was pulled into a severe bun, but her face was warm and friendly.

"Madam Hastings." She held out her hand. "My name is Doctor Fontaine, but please call me Charlotte."

Victoria shook her hand. "Victoria."

Charlotte nodded and gestured for Victoria to follow her inside.

"Samuel tells me that you know Clémence?"

Victoria bristled at the alias. "Holly. Yes, I do."

"How is it that you know Holly?"

They entered the building, and the sharp smell of disinfectant caused Victoria to wince.

"She was my assistant," she replied succinctly. She wasn't interested in small talk, she wanted to see Holly as soon as possible and find out what was going on.

"I see," Charlotte said. "And why was she in France?"

"Fashion Week."

Charlotte lifted the plastic card that hung from a lanyard around her neck. It connected with a device on the door, and a green light shone. She pushed the door open and walked into an office where she gestured for Victoria to sit down.

"She did not travel back to America with you?" Charlotte asked.

Victoria looked around the office in frustration.

"Holly terminated her employment with my magazine during Fashion Week last year. We didn't see her again," she explained. She stood in the doorway, making it clear that she had no intention of sitting down.

"I see. Was there a disagreement?" Charlotte asked.

"No, there was no disagreement. Do you intend to continue this cross-examination of me?"

Charlotte sat in her office chair and looked up at Victoria.

"I'm afraid so, yes. Clémence…" She held up her hands. "I apologise, Holly, is under my care. And has been for eleven months. She was admitted after suffering from a serious head injury, with no memory and no identification on her. As I'm sure you can understand, this caused us many issues when dealing with her medical treatment, with no medical history to go on, and no understanding of why she suffers memory loss. I need to find out if psychological trauma was a factor in her accident or her memory loss."

Victoria's eyes fluttered closed for a moment. She nodded.

"I apologise." She took the offered seat in front of the desk. "I understand. Holly decided to leave us last year. I don't completely understand why. One moment she was there, the next she was gone. We never heard from her again and assumed that she had left and returned to America on her own. It was quite a shock when Monsieur Durand showed me her photograph."

Charlotte looked sympathetic. "I imagine it was. Tell me, do you know of any accident or any medical history that could explain her amnesia?"

Victoria shook her head. "No. She was in perfect health when I last saw her. As far as I was aware, anyway."

Charlotte leaned back in her chair. She toyed with the pen in her hands while looking at Victoria critically.

"Forgive me for saying so, but your reputation leads me

to believe that maybe your staff would be, shall we say, unlikely to confide in you?"

Victoria pursed her lips. It was a fair assessment but not one she enjoyed hearing.

"I suppose that is true," she allowed. "But I'm still generally aware of my staff and their health and wellbeing."

It wasn't entirely true. She hadn't noticed when Louise had pneumonia and was eventually carted off to the hospital in an ambulance, but Charlotte didn't need to know that.

"How would you describe your relationship with Holly?"

Victoria tensed. She hadn't felt under such scrutiny in a long time. She'd become used to doors naturally opening for her the moment she approached them. Her position usually allowed her anything she desired. Right now, she had a desperate need to see Holly but the gatekeeper wasn't being cooperative. She knew that her usual strategy of demands and bullishness wasn't going to work.

"We worked side by side for seven months. She was my assistant and, as such, she was closer to me than most. In fact, during that time I probably saw more of Holly than I did my own children."

It was the truth, but it didn't mean they were close. Victoria simply worked damn hard.

Charlotte leaned forward. She put the pen back down on her desk and looked at Victoria.

Victoria knew she was being analysed. She knew the look well, she used it herself to great effect. But she analysed magazine layouts, editorial photography, fashion trends. Charlotte analysed people. And that unnerved her.

"Have you ever spoken with someone who suffers from

memory loss?"

"No," Victoria said. "I'm afraid my knowledge is drawn solely from popular media, which I assume is not entirely accurate."

Charlotte chuckled softly. "You are right. Unfortunately, the depictions you see in television and movies are not at all accurate. I must warn you that it can be very difficult to speak with someone with no memory of you."

Victoria felt her frame loosen slightly with relief. It seemed that she was passing Charlotte's entrance exam.

"I'm sure it is," she agreed. "May I ask of her condition? How much of her memory is lost? Will her memories return?"

Charlotte leaned back in her chair again. She was the picture of defeat. Victoria realised that they had something in common; they were both protective of Holly. Charlotte was standing in between her and Holly, but Victoria knew that if their positions were reversed, she would do exactly the same.

"It is difficult to say," Charlotte admitted. "The type of memory loss she has is very unusual. Usually with brain trauma, we see a tendency for future memories to become lost or muddled. Patients can often remember their past but have difficulty correctly recording and cataloguing events following the trauma."

"But that isn't what is happening here?" Victoria guessed.

"Indeed. With Holly, we see the opposite. Her memories before the incident are gone. Despite how often this type of memory loss appears on film, it is very rare in real life."

"So, she doesn't remember her past?"

Charlotte shook her head. "She remembers nothing. Not her name, her family. Her first memory is of waking up in the hospital after her accident."

"What was this accident?"

"We do not know. She was taken to the accident and emergency department of a local hospital after being found by a police officer on the side of the road."

Victoria clenched her hands over the arms of the chair.

"But we do not know what happened," Charlotte continued. "Nor can we tell if the accident caused her memory loss. There is a possibility that something happened prior to the accident, causing her memory loss and therefore causing the accident."

"I take it the not knowing makes treatment difficult?"

"We know very little about the brain," Charlotte said. "There are no medications that can cure memory loss. It's a matter of whether or not the brain will repair itself. Or if it can. The part of the brain responsible for storing those memories may have been damaged, or possibly have disappeared altogether as a result of the damage. Our knowledge of memory centres is very small. What we don't know far outweighs what we do."

Victoria swallowed. The enormity of what had happened was starting to settle in her mind. She suspected it would take a while to fully grasp the situation, what they currently knew of it anyway. It seemed that there were a lot of unknowns.

"May I see her?"

Charlotte stood and gestured towards the office door. "Please, follow me."

CHAPTER FIVE

As the taxi started to slow, Gideon Fisher looked over the top of his newspaper. He'd been so engrossed in an article that he hadn't noticed that they had arrived at the airport. He folded the paper and grabbed his Ted Baker briefcase.

The passenger door flew open. His head snapped up in shock.

"Victoria's gone AWOL," Louise announced. "And where have you been? I've been trying to contact you."

Gideon ignored the hyperactive woman and leaned forward to tap his bank card on the payment machine. He gestured for Louise to stand back with a shooing motion and exited the car. The taxi driver unloaded his luggage from the boot.

"*Merci*," Gideon said.

He pulled up the suitcase handle and attached his briefcase to it. He slid the newspaper into the front pocket and patted his coat down to ensure he had everything he needed.

"Right. Now, let's have that again, from the start?" he requested.

"Where's your phone?" Louise demanded. She waved her own phone about. "I've called you a million times."

"Impressive," he said, raising his eyebrow. It wasn't unusual for Louise to become agitated. "My phone is updating, some software thing that—"

"Never mind that," Louise said. "Victoria is AWOL. Missing. Lost!"

Gideon raised his arm and looked at his watch. There was still time before the flight.

"Her driver didn't show up. I called him, but he hardly speaks any English. He said he dropped her off somewhere, but I couldn't make out where."

"Okay." Gideon lowered his arm. "Have you tried calling her?"

"Of course I have," Louise sighed. "No answer."

Gideon shrugged. He grabbed the handle of his suitcase and started to walk towards the departures terminal. "Well, there's not a lot you can do at the moment. There's still time before we need to call the National Guard, or whomever you call in a situation like this."

Louise fell into step behind him.

"But this isn't on the schedule," she complained.

"It's not the first time Victoria has changed her schedule," Gideon reminded her. "Maybe a meeting opportunity came up? It's Paris Fashion Week, remember? Anyone who's anyone is here. She'll want to maximise every moment of her time."

"I ordered her brunch," Louise said. "Do I tell the chef that she isn't coming?"

Gideon sighed. "I have no idea. Which is why I'm grateful that looking after Victoria's schedule is your job and not mine."

He offered her a half-sympathetic smile and walked towards the check-in desk.

CHAPTER SIX

Victoria followed Dr Charlotte Fontaine through the hospital's in-patient recreation room. She'd never felt so out of place in her life. Her expensive couture was at odds with a room filled with people wearing what could generously be described as loungewear.

Her heels clicked loudly on the linoleum flooring, causing patients to look at her as she passed. She tried not to make eye contact with any of them.

In the corner of the room was a table. Three chairs around the table were unoccupied. The remaining chair faced away from Victoria, but she knew its occupant was Holly.

As they got closer, she could see that the girl was reading a book. Charlotte took the seat opposite Holly and gestured for Victoria to sit between them. Victoria was grateful that Holly was looking at Charlotte as she sat down. She was sure her usual neutral mask had slipped upon seeing Holly. The short hair and unhealthy pallor were shocking to see in person.

"Bonjour, Clémence. How are you today?" Charlotte asked.

Holly smiled and laid her book down on the table. Victoria noted that it was a moth-eaten copy of *Moby Dick*.

"I'm good, thank you."

Four simple words, so common in everyday conversation, struck fear into Victoria's heart. There wasn't a trace of recognition from Holly. She didn't sound like herself, she sounded hollow.

Victoria wasn't sure if she believed in the concept of a soul, but if she had to explain Holly's demeanour in that moment, it would be as if hers were missing.

"*Bon*," Charlotte replied. She gestured to Victoria. "This is Victoria."

Holly turned to look at Victoria and held out her hand.

"Nice to meet you," Holly said, a polite smile on her face.

Victoria stalled for a moment before shaking her hand.

"Likewise," she said simply.

Holly retracted her hand and looked back at Charlotte. Confusion was clear in her expression as she waited for an explanation.

Victoria looked down at her own hand. She realised that it was probably the first time she had ever come into direct physical contact with Holly.

Charlotte gestured to Victoria, encouraging Holly to face her again.

"Do you recognise Victoria?" Charlotte enquired casually.

Holly turned to look at her again.

Victoria held herself taut. It was the first time any of her assistants had ever looked at her with such a probing eye. Most of her staff, Holly included, avoided eye contact at all costs. It felt strange to be under such scrutiny, especially from someone who had formerly been so timid.

"I'm sorry," Holly addressed Victoria politely. "I don't remember anything from before a year ago. I had an accident. Did we meet?"

Victoria felt her face contort into a supportive half-smile. She had felt for sure that Holly would take one look at her and would experience some kind of total recall. She'd recoil in horror, but at least her memories would be intact.

"Do you think you've met?" Charlotte asked before Victoria could speak.

Holly looked at Victoria again. Her eyes scanned her face, her hair, her clothes, looking for anything of consequence that might jog a memory. She looked back to Charlotte with a sad shake of her head.

"I don't know, I'm sorry."

"No need to apologise." Charlotte smiled warmly. She stood up. "I'm going to leave you two to get reacquainted. Call me if you need me, I'll be right over there."

Victoria's heart nearly stopped. Before she had a chance to protest, Charlotte had stepped away. Still within earshot, but far enough away for Victoria to feel abandoned and under an intense spotlight.

Victoria looked at Holly. She opened her mouth and then closed it again, unsure of what to say.

"So," Holly started, "do you… do you know me?"

"Yes," Victoria breathed.

"Can you tell me… about… well… me? Like, my name?" Holly asked.

Holly's desperate plea shook the cobwebs from her mind. Whether or not she wanted to be here, she was, and she was all Holly had. She needed to step up.

"Yes, of course, your name is Holly Carter."

The girl's eyes widened. "Holly," she murmured.

Victoria watched the young woman in astonishment as she whispered her name to herself over and over, testing the feel of it on her tongue.

"I'm sorry, what did you say your name was?" Holly asked.

"Victoria. Victoria Hastings." She wondered if the name might jog a memory.

"Holly," the young woman mumbled again. "Victoria Hastings and Holly… what was it again?"

"Carter."

Holly nodded and stared at the table. Her forehead furrowed, and she appeared deep in thought. After a few moments she shook her head in frustration.

"No, nothing. I'm so sorry."

Victoria's hand darted across the table and captured Holly's before she had time to consider what she was doing.

"Don't apologise, there's absolutely no need for you to be sorry."

Holly smiled, still uncertain but starting to become more confident. She squeezed Victoria's hand gently before retracting her own.

"So, are you… I mean.. are we… related? Or…?" Holly looked uncertain.

"We… worked together," Victoria said. She wasn't sure how much she wanted to give away just yet. She knew Holly needed the information, but she wanted to wait a little while longer before the inevitable distance was thrown up between them again.

Holly slowly nodded. "Where do... *did* we work?"

"*Arrival*, an international fashion magazine. I am the New York editor-in-chief and you... were... my second assistant."

Holly couldn't have looked more surprised if Victoria had told her that she was an astronaut. As the information sunk in, she let out a small giggle.

"So... I'm a fashion person?"

Victoria chuckled lightly at the very thought.

"No, you were most definitely not a *fashion person*, Holly. You came to work for me because you were interested in writing, editorials and journalism. You were a temp who became a permanent member of staff after my previous second assistant left. I believe you were hoping to move to the writing staff in the future, or to one of our sister publications."

Holly smiled. "Phew, I thought I'd lost more than my memory for a moment. I mean, I can tell you're into all that fashion stuff, but I don't think that's me."

Victoria allowed the phrase *fashion stuff* to go by with merely a tiny wince.

Holly suddenly slapped her hand across her mouth. Her eyes were wide, realisation dawning.

"You're my boss!"

Victoria nodded.

"Yes, I am... well..." She hesitated for a moment, debated whether she should mention Holly's vanishing act. It occurred to her that this new information could explain

Holly's sudden departure. Maybe the girl hadn't up and quit her job after all.

"Yes, I'm your boss."

"And you have two assistants?" Holly questioned.

"Yes." Victoria nodded.

"So, you're kind of a big deal?" Holly asked.

Victoria dismissed the question with a small flick of her wrist. "Never mind that now, Holly. We need to focus on you, not me."

Holly slowly nodded. Victoria could see the cogs of her mind working overtime.

"Do I have any family? Am I married? Do I have kids? What about my mom and dad?"

Victoria blinked at the onslaught of questions. She swallowed, realising again that she was probably the worst person in the world to be doing this.

"You're not married, as far as I'm aware. And no children. I'm afraid I don't know about your parents, we never really spoke of..." She paused. She wanted to say that they had never spoken of anything personal. She wanted to clarify their relationship. Wanted to advise Holly that she had had the misfortune of coming across the least helpful person possible.

"I suppose I always knew that I didn't have anyone," Holly said. "I mean, no one ever came looking for me. And the guy from the embassy said that no one had reported me missing."

Victoria had no idea how to respond to that. It seemed so wrong that Holly had been left to fend for herself in a foreign country. Recovering in a hospital with the knowledge that no one had missed her presence.

"So, do I live in New York?"

Victoria felt relief at the arrival of a question she could answer with certainty.

"Yes, you live in the city."

"Wow…" Holly smiled, her head tilted as she took that piece of information in. "I wonder if I still have a place there. I wonder where my stuff is? I must have had stuff?"

"Yes, you must have had 'stuff'," Victoria agreed.

Samuel approached the table. "Hello, Clémence."

Holly jumped up and hugged the man. "Sam! Oh, Sam, did you do this? Did you find Victoria?"

"Oui." He stepped back, a wide smile on his face as he clutched Holly's hands in his. "I had nearly given up. And suddenly I saw you on television."

Holly's eyes shone with surprise. "Me? On television?"

"Yes." He nodded. "You and Victoria. I only saw you for a second, but I knew it was you. It was a news article about Fashion Week. They were showing some footage from the previous year, and there you were. Beside this wonderful lady here."

Victoria felt herself blush as he nodded in her direction.

Holly threw her arms around him again. "I cannot thank you enough!"

Victoria felt uncomfortable and used the opportunity to make her escape. She stood up. "Excuse me, I need to speak with Dr Fontaine."

Holly took a step back from Samuel and looked at Victoria, her eyes flashing with fear.

"I will be right back, I just need to speak with your doctor," she reassured. "I won't be leaving."

Holly nodded, a fearful look remaining on her face.

Samuel put his arm around her and gestured to the book on the table.

"*Moby Dick*, again?" he asked.

Holly and Samuel sat down at the table and spoke with each other.

Victoria made eye contact with Charlotte. The doctor nodded her head and indicated a corridor off of the recreation room where they could speak privately.

Once they were away from prying ears, Victoria spoke. "I'm not a medical expert, but twelve months is a very long time for someone to still be in the hospital. She doesn't appear to be ill, aside from the memory loss. I'm surprised that she is still here."

Charlotte leaned against the wall, her arms folded across her chest. "Yes, when she first arrived, she was in emergency care for a month while she recovered from the accident. For the next six months, she was here for therapy to recover her motor skills—"

"Motor skills?" Victoria questioned.

"It's not unusual for brain trauma patients to need to relearn basic motor functions. Walking, eating, drinking, writing. Luckily Clémence—apologies, Holly—recovered these skills quickly. For other skills, she is still receiving therapy. This, coupled with the fact that the system here is very slow, means that Holly has remained here while our board decided where she would go and who would care for her."

"Care for her?"

"Yes, she's unable to care for herself. Her motor functions are still not one hundred percent. She had no knowledge of the French language other than basic phrases. Part of her treatment has been to immerse her in her native language. The American authorities could not identify her and therefore would not pay for her treatment. The French authorities wanted the Americans to take responsibility for her wellbeing. Holly has been stuck in a very long game of political Ping-Pong. She has remained here while the legal issues are outstanding."

Victoria could well believe the scenario Charlotte described. She'd dipped her toe into the political world on occasion, only to be horrified at the amount of red tape that greeted her.

"How do I resolve this? How can I get her home?"

Charlotte let out a long breath. "Well, that would be very difficult. You would need to prove who she is. That way she can be released from the care of the French medical system. Then there would need to be a decision made regarding her ability to travel, we would need to be sure that someone would care for her on-going medical needs. We cannot simply let her go without knowing she will be cared for. If something were to happen, we could be held responsible."

Victoria leaned her back against the opposite wall and stared down at the floor. She was starting to realise the enormity of the situation.

"And, we must not forget," Charlotte continued, "that it is of course up to her, as well."

Victoria looked up.

"We cannot allow someone to take responsibility for her without her permission. She is mentally able to have a say. There are few people in the world she knows, never mind trusts," Charlotte said.

Victoria nodded. She turned to look into the recreation room where Samuel and Holly were deep in conversation. She started to have a small inkling of how lost and helpless Holly must have felt soon after the accident. Everything had changed, and everything was going to continue to change for a while longer yet.

She couldn't leave the girl behind again. She felt she was suffocating with guilt already. There was no way that she would be leaving Paris without her former second assistant.

CHAPTER SEVEN

"Just think of the peace and quiet you'll have," Gideon said, watching Louise with no great concern. She sat on an uncomfortable airport terminal chair, head between her legs, breathing into a brown paper bag.

"You can take Victoria's seat in first class... actually, scratch that, that would put you next to me. You can keep your own seat in premium, relaxed in the knowledge that —"

"Relaxed?!" Louise crumpled the paper bag and glared up at him. "Relaxed? Are you insane? Victoria is gone. She will miss her flight, and who will she blame for that? Me. That's who. She will blame me for missing her flight and throwing her entire schedule off. Gideon, this is a complete disaster."

"Victoria is a grown woman. If she's gone off somewhere, then she knows she'll miss her flight," Gideon reasoned.

"Oh, come on." Louise stood up and started to pace. "Remember the time we were in London and she demanded that the plane leave twenty minutes early so she'd be able to get an earlier connection to take Hugo to a concert?"

Gideon laughed. That did sound familiar, but he was so used to Victoria's behaviour by now that it all blended into the background. Of course, he didn't have to deal with her whims on a daily basis either.

Louise's phone rang in the distinctive tune that was assigned to Victoria. And Lord Vader. She ran for her bag and tipped the contents onto the chair. She grabbed the phone and swiped at the screen.

"Hello? Victoria?"

Louise's face contorted in confusion.

"What? Um. You… Yes, I-I'll see what I can do. Yes, yes, right away. What about your flight—" She pulled her phone away from her ear and looked at the screen. "She hung up."

"What did she say?" Gideon asked.

Louise looked at him. "You won't believe this, but she wants me to get a copy of Holly Carter's passport."

Gideon blinked. "Holly's passport?" It had been a long time since that name had been uttered.

"Yep. She didn't say why. Just that she wants it emailed to her immediately." Louise stood rooted to the spot in confusion. "Why on earth does she want that traitor's passport? What's going on?"

Gideon got his own phone out of his inner jacket pocket and scrolled to Victoria's number.

"Who knows? Just do what she says. Call human resources and ask them to get a copy out of the file," he told her. "And tell them to hurry up. Whatever it is, she won't want to be kept waiting."

Louise snapped out of her daze and started to swipe through her contact list.

Gideon walked away from where they had been sitting and dialled Victoria. A few moments went by before the call was answered.

"Victoria? What's going on?" he asked.

"Gideon, you wouldn't believe me if I told you," she said through a sigh.

"You just asked Louise to get a copy of Holly's passport?"

"Don't tell the masses, and certainly don't tell Louise, I want to keep this quiet for now," Victoria said. "Holly is here, in France."

Gideon couldn't quite work out the connection. "And… she's lost her passport?"

"She's lost everything. She's in a hospital," Victoria whispered.

Gideon turned away from the crowds of the terminal and faced a nearby wall in an attempt to hide his shock.

"In a hospital? Is she okay?"

"She has severe memory loss, she doesn't know who she is," Victoria explained.

"How on earth did you find her?"

"That's a long story, for another day. Suffice to say, I'm staying here with her until I can get this mess sorted out. I need a copy of her passport in order to prove her identity and get the wheels in motion to bring her home."

Gideon leaned his arm against the wall. "Yes, yes, I see. Is there anything I can do?"

"Actually, there is. You used to speak to Holly, didn't you? I saw you two whispering to each other often. Do you know much about Holly's family? Parents? Siblings? Does she have a boyfriend? I really don't know what to tell her. I knew so little about her."

He stood up straight and started to walk. He felt so cut off and useless that movement was the only thing keeping him from going insane.

"Well, her parents died in a car crash about six years ago. No brothers or sisters that she's ever spoken about. No boyfriend, but she broke up with her long-term girlfriend just before she left for Paris. They were having difficulties and Holly made the break. I think she intended to return from Paris and get her life back on track." He snorted a bitter laugh. "She had a couple of friends she spoke about fairly regularly, but she had a big falling out with them when she left her girlfriend."

He heard a deep sigh from Victoria. "Don't you have anything… positive? Something I can tell her that doesn't sound so dire?"

Gideon searched his memory for the last few weeks of conversations he'd had with Holly.

"Nothing that springs to mind," he admitted. "She was at a crossroads in her life. Making a lot of changes. She loved her job and was looking forward to starting a career in writing. Everything else was falling away as she focused on her career."

"I see," Victoria replied. "Well, at least I have something to tell her, I suppose. Please keep this between us, but tell Louise to hurry up with that passport."

CHAPTER EIGHT

Victoria disconnected the call. She summoned a deep and calming breath. This day certainly wasn't working out in the way she had planned.

Worst of all, she couldn't tell Louise what was happening. If she did, the entire *Arrival* staff, worldwide, would know. They'd know that Victoria hadn't followed up on Holly's departure and had instead abandoned the girl. The story would quickly grow into Victoria having somehow caused the brain trauma personally. She could see it now, secretaries taking bets on how it was done, like a winning guess in *Clue*: Victoria with the hole punch at the Vuitton preview.

She was dealing with quite enough without having to endure the gossip pool as well. Telling Louise was out of the question. Which meant she was effectively without an assistant and would have to deal with all of Holly's paperwork herself.

She left the room where she had been making calls and returned to the recreation room. She crossed back towards the table where Holly and Samuel continued their conversation.

As she approached, Holly looked up at her and smiled. Victoria found herself uncharacteristically returning the smile. She could see some of the brightness returning to Holly's eyes. A sliver of her former self seemed to be returning.

Samuel stood up and held out a card. Victoria took it, it looked like a business card that had been printed at home.

"Merci," he said, "for speaking to me earlier today. And for everything. Please let me know that she is okay."

"I will keep you updated," Victoria said as she pocketed the business card.

Holly stood up and hugged him farewell. He said a final goodbye to Victoria and walked away.

Holly watched him leave. "I wonder what would have happened without him," she wondered.

"He certainly is persistent," Victoria said.

Holly looked at Victoria nervously. "So, what happens now?"

Victoria gestured for Holly to sit down as she did the same. She straightened her spine and looked Holly in the eye. This was a serious discussion, one that had to go perfectly. There could be no doubts, no misunderstandings, and no concerns. In short, Victoria had to do things that she wasn't particularly good at. Mainly, explain herself and be sympathetic to someone else's thoughts and feelings.

"What happens next is somewhat up to you," Victoria admitted. "I am getting a copy of your passport sent over to me. That will allow us to prove who you are and that you're an American citizen. Once that happens, the French authorities will release you into the care of the American authorities—"

"I don't want to go back to the American Embassy," Holly interrupted. "They weren't very nice, and they didn't help me at all."

"The hospital won't discharge you unless you are legally under someone's care, at least for the immediate future," Victoria explained gently. "That won't be the embassy. In fact, I'd like to take on that role in order to get you home to New York. So that you can get settled again. I understand that may be a little difficult as we've only just met…"

Holly looked around the room as she slowly nodded. "I'd like to leave here. And maybe I'll remember something when I see New York?"

"Maybe you will," Victoria said, trying to keep things light without providing the girl with any false hope. "Would you like to be discharged into my care?"

Holly looked to Victoria and opened her mouth to speak.

"Apologies for eavesdropping," Charlotte said as she appeared by their table and sat down.

"Understandable," Victoria commented. She gestured for the doctor to continue.

"Clémence, are you comfortable with this? Once you leave the hospital you will not be able to return to us."

"Holly," Victoria muttered.

Holly ignored Victoria, focusing her attention on Charlotte. "I want to go back to New York. I might remember who I am. Or at least recognise something. I've been here forever, and everything still seems alien to me."

"Going back to New York may help your memories to

return, but, as we discussed before, there is a real possibility that those memories are gone forever."

"I know," Holly said softly. "But I want to try."

"I understand," Charlotte said. "Are you comfortable with Victoria having power of attorney for you and your affairs?"

Victoria picked up her phone from the table top and started to check her email messages. She didn't want Holly to feel pressured, even though she desperately wanted – no, *needed* – the girl to say yes.

"I-I don't know what that means," Holly confessed.

"It means that she will be legally responsible for you, for your well-being. You maintain control, but she can make decisions on your behalf that will directly affect you. She can manage your financial affairs, she can make limited decisions regarding your medical treatment, and she can decide where you live. As you have sustained a brain trauma, there may be other powers she has, so you may want to consult a legal advisor regarding the laws in America."

Victoria gripped her phone a little tighter. She may have been endeavouring to look like she was not paying attention, but Charlotte's words hit her like a freight train. She hadn't taken into consideration the complexities of Holly's care.

She started to wonder if she should be more open with the girl. Maybe she should explain that she was considered the most difficult woman to work for in all of North America. Maybe she should hint at the number of times her unreasonable demands had previously reduced Holly to tears.

And then there was the matter of Holly's departure. One moment she had been there, the next she hadn't. Before today, Victoria had assumed that the girl had quit her job and walked away. She'd been a monster throughout Fashion Week the previous year. It had felt possible, even probable, that Holly had quit as a result.

Now the timeline was muddied. Maybe Holly had quit. Or maybe she had walked away to take a breath with every intention of returning later. Although her room had been emptied of her belongings when Victoria had hammered on the door a few hours later, nothing was certain. Whatever had happened, the fact remained: Victoria had driven the mild-mannered woman to abandon her post.

But Victoria feared that any amount of honesty at this point would ruin everything. She already felt that she had less than a fingertip grip on the girl. She wasn't willing to loosen that hold further.

A new email from Louise flashed up on her screen. Victoria opened it and scanned through the contents. Apparently, she had managed to wake the head of human resources and asked them to either log into the archives remotely or to go into the office early and immediately send a copy of Holly's file to her and Victoria.

Oh, heaven help her. The girl had even used the word *stat*.

The impossible now seemed a little closer. Victoria smiled to herself and looked up with the intention of rejoining the conversation.

Holly looked deep in thought as she stared out of the window.

"This isn't a decision to rush into," Charlotte said. "There is no hurry."

Victoria felt her tightly-packed schedule slipping through her fingers. She was already aware that missing her flight to New York was going to have a knock-on effect. She wanted to say that there was a hurry, but she knew that patience would win the battle.

"I think I should go," Holly said. "I want to go home. If that's okay with you, Victoria?"

"Absolutely." Victoria turned to Charlotte. "A member of my staff is currently sourcing Holly's passport, I should have it within the next hour. What do we do from there?"

"I need to speak with our legal team. Once we have the passport, we'll need to draw up a power of attorney and have it signed by a judge. That will take some time." Charlotte sighed.

"How much time?" Victoria asked.

"I'm not sure, at least three days," Charlotte said.

"That's unacceptable," Victoria snarled. "This will be completed today. I have already missed my flight to New York for today, but I fully intend for us to both be on the same flight tomorrow."

Both Holly and Charlotte looked at Victoria in surprise. Holly more so than Charlotte.

Charlotte stood up. "Of course, I will speak with my legal team in order to start proceedings immediately. I cannot guarantee any speed in the matter. Our courts are notoriously slow and that is, unfortunately, out of my hands."

"I will ensure that feet are not dragged," Victoria promised.

Charlotte nodded and left the two women alone. Victoria's gaze settled on Holly to find that the girl was looking at her with a half-smirk.

"What?" Victoria asked.

"Nothing." The smirk became a smile.

"That kind of delay is uncalled for," Victoria explained. "The French are so lax. If you give them an inch, they'll take a mile."

"I agree. Dealing with them so far hasn't been great."

Victoria was pleased that Holly hadn't reacted badly to her outburst, although she suspected that was because she was on the right side of it. In the past, such outbursts would have sent Holly scuttling to fix whatever mess had befallen her.

"So, what does a second assistant do?"

Victoria sat back a little, surprised at the question. The truth was, she had no idea what a second assistant did. She had no idea precisely what either of her assistants did, other than ensure her office ran with the clockwork precision she demanded.

"Assist the first assistant, who assists me," Victoria finally responded. It wasn't entirely true. Once Holly had proved herself, Victoria had taken to going directly to Holly with her requests and cutting Louise out of the loop entirely. But there was no need to get into that now.

"So, I'm pretty low on the food chain?"

Victoria blanched. "Absolutely not. You're second assistant to the editor-in-chief of *Arrival* Magazine. A million girls would kill for your job."

Holly's expression became distant.

"What is it?" Victoria asked.

"I'm… I'm just wondering why you didn't report me missing?" Holly looked at her. "I mean… I'm just trying to piece together what happened."

Victoria swallowed. The entire situation was difficult, but this moment, in particular, was one she dreaded.

"Well, you vanished, and we suspected that you had quit. The day before we were due to return home, you walked away from me. One moment you were there, the next minute you weren't."

Holly's eyes widened in shock and she raised a hand to cover her open mouth.

"Later, I went to your room in the hotel and your things were gone. Naturally, I thought you had left and gone home."

Victoria started to recall the events of that night. She had expected Holly to reappear, apologetic and embarrassed by her actions. But when she didn't, Victoria's anger had built to a crescendo. At the end of a packed day, she returned to the hotel and hammered on Holly's hotel room door.

She'd expected to find Holly in her room, awaiting hell and begging forgiveness. Eventually, she used the spare keycard she had been given in case of emergency and was shocked to find the room had been emptied.

A quick search of the wardrobe and the bathroom confirmed that Holly had left. Victoria had sat on the edge of the perfectly made bed, replaying the last conversation she had with the girl for clues.

A mere half-hour passed before Victoria left the room, but the feeling of loss and later anger remained for a long time.

"I'm so sorry, I don't know why on earth I would have done that." Holly shook her head. "It doesn't sound like me. Well, I don't think it does."

"It's done now." Victoria offered a small shrug.

Holly hadn't been the first person to leave her, nor would she be the last. If anything, Victoria was at fault for letting the girl slip so stealthily under her defences.

A nurse walked up to Holly, and Holly looked at the clock on the wall with surprise.

"Oh, wow, is that the time already?" She looked at Victoria apologetically. "I… um… I have a physiotherapy appointment."

Victoria could see fear flash in Holly's eyes. Fear of abandonment, she presumed. She recognised it well.

"Then I can occupy myself by calling my lawyer and setting the wheels in motion to get you home. I'll head to my hotel, but I'll be back this evening to update you and tell you what our plan of action is."

Holly looked relieved, though still uncertain. "Thank you, I-I can't thank you enough."

"No need to thank me," Victoria told her. "Go and have your appointment. I'll be back later."

Holly looked at her for a moment, uncertainty clear in her eyes. Eventually she nodded and stood up, accompanied by the staff member.

A moment after Holly left, Charlotte returned.

"How are you doing?" Charlotte asked.

"It's all rather difficult to take in," Victoria admitted.

"It is, and it will be," Charlotte agreed. "There's nothing that can prepare you for a situation like this."

"That's certainly true. How intensive is the physiotherapy?"

"She currently has a two-hour session each day, as well as another two hours of memory building and retrieval exercises. Both these treatments will need to be continued when she returns to America."

"Of course," Victoria said. In her mind, she was already planning the best way to organise Holly's treatments. Naturally, she'd be seeing the best doctors in New York.

Charlotte took a piece of paper out of the deep pocket of her lab coat and handed it to Victoria.

"Here are the details of our legal manager. She will be able to speak with your legal advisor to make arrangements."

Victoria glanced at the information before dropping the paper into her handbag.

"I shall return to my hotel and make the necessary arrangements. I promised Holly that I would return this evening." She wasn't asking permission.

Victoria was rapidly running out of patience with the entire process. She was beyond the shock of seeing Holly and now wanted to process the legal side of things as quickly as possible.

She handed a business card to Charlotte as she stood up.

"My contact details," she explained. "Thank you for all you've done. I hope you don't find it disrespectful of me to say that I hope we can resolve this matter quickly."

Charlotte stood as well and gestured towards the corridor they'd entered from.

"Absolutely not disrespectful. My primary goal is, and

has always been, Holly's care. I'm sure that we can work together to ensure everything moves smoothly."

It didn't escape Victoria's notice that Charlotte wasn't making any promises as to the future. She hoped that the doctor wouldn't prove too much of an obstacle. While she'd initially been concerned about being allowed access to Holly, now her trepidation had melted and been replaced by determination.

Now that she had seen Holly, she wouldn't stop until she brought the girl home. Money and legal expertise would not be spared in her quest to do so.

It was no longer a matter of *if* Victoria would bring the girl home, but *when*.

CHAPTER NINE

Gideon covered the mouthpiece of his mobile with his hand and leaned towards Louise.

"Call the Shangri-La, tell them to get the presidential suite ready for Victoria. She's on her way back there now," he whispered.

Louise grabbed her phone and dutifully swiped at the screen.

He returned his attention to the call.

"I'll need you to speak with Edmond, obviously," Victoria was saying. "And we need to do something about the cosmetics layout. Speak to Stella—"

"Sheila," Gideon corrected.

"Mm, that one, and tell her no to the greys, we need warmth. Try to do something about the budget preparations; I may be a genius, but I don't know how I'm supposed to put out a Christmas edition with anything less than four hundred thousand. Tell Louise to prepare my guestroom, I'll need everything, obviously."

"Your guestroom?" Gideon questioned.

"Yes, Holly will have to stay with me. We can't have her roaming the streets of New York, can we?"

Gideon smiled at Victoria's dramatization. "I thought you'd put her in a hotel."

"That would be wholly inconvenient. Besides, we know she's not good at staying in hotels. The last time she stayed in a hotel, she got herself into the mess she's in now! No. She'll stay with me. Besides, if I'm going to be legally responsible for her, I need to be able to keep an eye on her."

"Legally responsible?"

"Yes, please keep up, Gideon." Victoria let out a sigh. "If I'm to get her out of that hole, then I need to have power of attorney."

Gideon suspected the facility wasn't a hole but decided to keep quiet.

"I see," he said simply.

"What's that supposed to mean?"

"Nothing, just I see. I understand what you're saying," he clarified. "What else can I do?"

"That's all for now. I'll email you anything else that comes to me, and I'll liaise with Claudia in New York. I don't need to tell you that I don't want anyone knowing about this yet."

"Of course, my lips are sealed." He wasn't entirely sure how to keep events secret when Louise was about to be asked to speak with Victoria's household staff to set up the guestroom. There was no point in asking Victoria. She wouldn't be interested in the how, just the result.

He paused a moment. "How is she?"

"A shell," she replied honestly. "She's lost so much

weight, not that she didn't have a few pounds to shed, of course."

Gideon rolled his eyes. He'd never been a fan of Victoria's insistence that all women working at the *Arrival* offices were impossibly skinny. Everyone at the magazine had considered Holly Carter on the heavy side, but to the average onlooker she probably would have been thought of as slim.

"She doesn't remember me," Victoria continued.

"That must be a relief," Gideon mumbled.

"What's that supposed to mean?" she snapped.

"You know what it means, you and Holly weren't exactly close. The girl was a nervous wreck around you, justifiably so most of the time. It must be nice to speak to her when she's not in the middle of heart palpitations."

A *tsk* was the only reply he got.

As director of photography, Gideon often had to liaise with Victoria's office. Louise was a frantic mess half of the time, and so he usually communicated with Holly instead. She had been a breath of fresh air, someone from outside the fashion world.

"You should come to the house for dinner one night when she is settled. Maybe she will remember you," Victoria suggested.

"Maybe. Whatever the outcome, I'd like to see her."

"I'll make the arrangements. I should go. You wouldn't believe the legal hoops I'm being forced to jump through."

Gideon imagined the exceptional situation probably called for some legal hoops but decided to not mention it.

"Good luck, I'll contact you when we land," he said.

As soon as he hung up the call, Louise appeared beside him.

"What is going on?" she demanded.

"Nothing that you need to know about at the moment," he told her.

He looked up at the departure board and then at his watch.

"Come on, we need to get to the gate," he said.

"Is this about Holly? What about the schedule? What's happening?" Louise asked.

"Cancel the schedule for the next few days. Yes, it's because of Holly, but don't ask any further questions because I can't tell you. Suffice to say, you're going to really earn your paycheck over the next few days."

CHAPTER TEN

Victoria waited patiently while the waiter wheeled in the lunch and tea she had ordered upon checking back into the Shangri-La. He removed each item from the trolley and arranged it carefully on her suite's dining room table.

Behind him, a widescreen television showed a man smothering a yawn. The moment she had arrived she had woken Michael in New York and demanded an immediate Skype conference. As her lawyer, he was used to such demands and didn't express irritation or surprise at her command.

Finally, the waiter seemed to realise that he was interrupting an important conversation and rushed from the room, the service trolley squeaking as he did.

The moment the suite door closed, Victoria let out a sigh and returned to where she had been standing in front of the television. The little square at the bottom right showing her irritated posture.

"You'd think the Shangri-La would have some oil for that trolley," Michael commented.

"They've been sent to try me." She pinched the bridge of her nose. "Where were we?"

"I was saying that my guy in London will be with you in a couple of hours." He smothered another yawn.

"Is that the best you can do, Michael?" She started to pace. "This really is of the utmost urgency. I need to fly back to New York as soon as possible."

"My guy in London is the best. He knows French and European law inside out. If getting back to New York is that pressing, then you can always leave your former assistant there and we'll deal with the legal details for you."

Victoria paused and glared at him. "*Leave her here*? Absolutely not! I promised her I would remain until this ridiculous mess is sorted out."

Michael chuckled.

"This is not funny," she told him darkly.

"No, it's not. But your reaction is a little amusing," he admitted. "Are you really sure you want to be responsible for power of attorney over this woman? It's a lot to ask of anyone, never mind someone with your workload."

Victoria rolled her eyes at the ceiling before pinning him with a glare.

"Yes, yes, I know all of that. I just need to get Holly out of that terrible facility."

Michael held up his iPad in his hand. "According to this report, it's one of the finest facilities in Europe. She was very lucky to be placed there."

Victoria snorted a laugh. "Don't believe everything you read online. I changed my own Wikipedia page to knock a few years off and no one batted an eyelid."

He lowered the iPad. "Regardless of the state of the hospital, we'll move as quickly as we can."

She walked over to the dining table, still in view of the camera mounted to the television. She picked up a cup and placed it on a saucer, then looked into the teapot to check if they had managed to get it right this time.

"What are the chances of expediting this matter?" she asked.

"We'll do our best, but the French courts are slow. To get her American identification officially recognised and name you as power of attorney, you will need to go to court. When Gareth gets there, he will set up an emergency appointment. Hopefully that will be this afternoon, but more likely first thing tomorrow morning. Once you have that, it's a matter of going to the American embassy and getting an emergency passport so that she can travel."

It sounded longwinded and exhausting. Victoria poured herself some tea. "And how long will an emergency passport take?"

"Same day, there's a walk-in service. As long as it isn't a weekend or a public holiday," he replied. "But I can't make any promises, this is very much out of our hands. And pushing them will just make the process slower."

Victoria's phone vibrated on the table, and she looked at the screen. HR had finally earned the redecoration of their offices.

"I have the photocopy of her passport," she told him. She forwarded the email to Michael. "I just sent it to you."

His iPad pinged. "Great, I have it. I'll send it to Gareth so he can speak to the embassy and get the ball rolling." He yawned again, swiping the screen to unlock it.

"Do you need anything else from me? I'm rather fed up with seeing your tonsils on a fifty-inch screen."

He chuckled. "Sorry, it's early here…"

"So everyone keeps informing me," she muttered.

"Oh," he said as he looked at his iPad.

She looked at him and frowned. "What?"

"Nice-looking girl." He looked at her over the top of his iPad, a cheeky look clear in his eyes.

Victoria shrugged. "I suppose she is."

"Mm." He waggled his eyebrows.

"Oh, go away," she told him.

"I'll get to it, don't worry. And Gareth will contact you when he arrives. He's very good, I have complete faith in him," Michael reassured her.

Victoria was still cross at being mocked. She simply shrugged her shoulders again and focused her attention on the lavish spread that the hotel had provided her.

"Good," she said simply.

"I'll contact you later," Michael said, wisely choosing to stop teasing her. He disconnected the call.

Victoria reached for the remote control and switched off the television. Her thirty-plus-year friendship with Michael often led to mutual teasing, but she suddenly found herself without a sense of humour. Her mind swam with questions, theories, and fears. Mostly fears.

Holly had been at the brunt of Victoria's moods ever since she started at *Arrival*. Someone with no understanding or care about fashion working for one of the most powerful women in fashion was laughable. Victoria had assumed she'd be gone within a week.

As they crossed the threshold into her second month of

employment, Victoria realised that Holly had staying power but still no interest in fashion. Sure, she'd improved her dress sense, but she was using the role as a segue into editorial. Not that that affected her determination. In fact, it made her one of the best assistants that Victoria had ever had.

Disastrously so.

Holly was always a few steps ahead of Victoria's needs. Ordering lunch, sending for cars, and booking meetings before she said a word.

While that should have been a dream come true, it was actually infuriating. Holly possessed an understanding of and familiarity with Victoria's needs that was distracting.

And so, Victoria rebelled.

The lunch was thrown in the trash, the car was cancelled, the meeting was delayed. Victoria tried to assert her authority, to not feel as transparent. She demeaned the girl, chastised her publicly, and sent her on ridiculous errands in the hope of her failing.

But Holly didn't back down. She redoubled her efforts to be everything Victoria needed and more. To be the best assistant.

They were stuck in a battle of wills, with one participant having no idea they were even at war.

And now the tables were turned. Holly would be utterly dependant on Victoria. She'd have control over her life, her finances, her living arrangements, and her medical treatment.

In her heart, she knew she hadn't been truthful at the hospital. While she hadn't outright lied, she hadn't been forthcoming with the truth. She hadn't explained to Holly who she was, what she was like, how she was feared and even hated at times. She certainly hadn't mentioned how Holly surely loathed her.

The knowledge that she may have found Holly only to lose her again, forever, was terrifying. And so, she shaped her own story. She omitted certain pieces of information from her conversations with both Charlotte and Holly.

Once the girl was safely home and recovering, then Victoria would show her true colours. Of course, there was a fine line to be walked. A balance to be had. She couldn't run the risk that Holly's memories might return before she had a chance to expose the truth of their relationship. Having power of attorney came with certain responsibilities, and honesty was one of them.

She speared a slice of apple from a plate and delicately bit into the flesh.

Still, she realised that she had time. Holly's memories wouldn't return in a flash, Charlotte had told her as much, which gave her the opportunity to be what Holly needed her to be. And if in the process she managed to cleanse her guilt, so be it.

CHAPTER ELEVEN

The grand building sparkled with polished glass and white marble. Victoria stepped into the wine bar and removed her oversized sunglasses. The floor manager quickly approached her.

"Madame Hastings, a pleasure. Your guest has already arrived."

He gestured to a booth at the back of the restaurant. She handed her coat and scarf to a waiter. She caught sight of her reflection in a gold-framed mirror and reached up to softly pat her fringe, ensuring that every hair laid correctly.

She approached the table, her hand out. "Gareth?"

Gareth Walker stood up and shook her hand. "Ms Hastings, nice to meet you."

"Victoria," she instructed.

She gestured for him to take his seat again and sat opposite him.

Michael had promised slick efficiency from his man in London. Victoria's eyes were drawn to his crumpled suit, askew tie, and messy hair. On the table were folders haphazardly stuffed with papers.

She hoped that appearances were deceptive.

"Would you like tea?" Victoria asked, eager to give the hovering waiter a task so they could get on with business.

Gareth nodded. "That sounds lovely."

Victoria turned to the waiter. "Tea," she ordered in a soft tone.

The waiter opened his mouth as if to ask a further question but thought better of it at her glare. He hurried away, and she turned back to Gareth expectantly.

"Thank you for agreeing to meet with me at such short notice," Gareth started. "I have been to the court and to the embassy, and I have scheduled in a few appointments for tomorrow."

Victoria maintained a neutral expression. She was already massively delayed. Even if Gareth snapped his fingers and produced the necessary signed documentation, a passport, and an airline ticket for a flight departing within the hour, it still wouldn't be enough to fix the damage that had already been done. If he was expecting a round of applause, he better have discovered a way to bend time.

"I have spoken with the hospital legal team, and all of the paperwork for the power of attorney has been prepared. We have a meeting with the French judge first thing in the morning. I intend that we will be done with that process around eleven. At midday, we have an appointment with the American Embassy. They have most of the passport application paperwork ready but will, of course, need to see and photograph Holly."

Victoria raised an eyebrow. It was looking more positive than she had expected.

"And when will the passport be issued?" she asked.

"Within half an hour, they just need to stamp the forms and then print it. They have most of it prepared. If you wish, you could book yourself a flight tomorrow afternoon and be back in New York in time for dinner."

Victoria sat back and pierced Gareth with a glare. "And then?"

Gareth frowned. "I'm sorry?"

"I was led to believe that this would be an enormous legal undertaking. You're telling me that both Holly and myself will be able to fly home tomorrow afternoon?"

Gareth picked up folder and flipped it open, searching through various official-looking documents. "There are a number of documents I need you to sign," he said. "And we must discuss the legal obligations when it comes to a power of attorney."

He pulled out a few papers and stacked them up.

Two waiters came by the table with trays filled with cups and saucers. They lowered the trays to the table and started to remove the items one by one.

Victoria shooed them away. "It's fine, we'll deal with it."

The waiters hurried away, and Victoria pushed the trays aside so they could continue to speak.

She leaned on the table. "But we're free to go tomorrow?" Victoria clarified.

"Yes, Michael explained that you needed this to be resolved as quickly as possible, so I leaned on a few contacts and pulled in a few favours."

She sat back and chuckled lightly. "I'm impressed."

"You haven't had the bill yet," Gareth muttered good-naturedly. He picked up a piece of paper and turned it around as he handed it to her.

"The price is irrelevant." She took the paper and winced. It was written in a font so small that only people in the legal profession were able to decipher it. She reached into her handbag and pulled out her reading glasses.

"I met with Holly this afternoon," Gareth said. "She seems a lovely girl, such a shame what happened to her. Whatever that was. It seems that there are parts of the puzzle we'll never know."

"Indeed," Victoria murmured. She wasn't in the mood for small talk. The paper she was reading seemed to form part of a document regarding the power of attorney. Judging by the fact that the sheet of paper was crammed with words, and seemed to only contain the opening statement, it would be a hefty document.

"So, you must have been close?" Gareth fished.

"She was my second assistant," Victoria replied without looking up.

She heard Gareth exhale lightly. "I'm not snooping. I need to deliver a statement to the court. The question as to why Holly was initially left in France, why no one followed up on her disappearance, and why you are now suddenly taking full legal responsibility for her is going to be raised."

Victoria lowered the document and glowered at him.

Gareth seemed completely unaffected by the stare that usually sent people running. He pulled a tea tray closer and prepared a cup for himself.

"I'm your legal representative," he explained. "You can tell me as little or as much as you like. You can also just tell me what you would like me to convey to the judge. I work for you. But whether it's the truth or a version of it, we need to come up with something that the judge will believe."

She placed the paper on the table and slowly removed her glasses, which she placed atop the document to better glare at Gareth.

"I'm sure you're aware of the rumours surrounding me," Victoria offered. "I'm not the easiest of people to work for."

"I've heard."

"Holly leaving my side last year was, in some ways, to be expected. My staff, especially my assistants, don't have the longest shelf life. She's not the first girl to walk away from me."

"And you didn't suspect it strange that she might do such a thing?" Gareth asked.

Victoria sniffed. "No. Well…" She paused and considered the question again. "Maybe. Assistants have left without notice in the past; suddenly deciding they don't want a job with opportunity and status, and leaving to do some menial task for someone I've never heard of. But prior to it actually happening, I would never have thought Holly capable of such a thing."

"So, you'd say it was out of character for her?"

Victoria leaned back and blew out a breath. "Maybe. We'd had a tense week. Though I hadn't pegged Holly as someone who would walk away from me when I needed her most, it had been a stressful week. I can see how the girl may have been on edge."

"Michael said her belongings were gone from the hotel?"

Victoria nodded. "Which indicates that she didn't snap,

walk away from me, and into an oncoming car around the corner."

"But she could have snapped, gone to the hotel, packed her things, and then been hit by a car," Gareth pointed out.

"We'll never know," Victoria said coldly.

She'd been over the events a hundred times in her mind. She didn't appreciate Gareth's input and theorising.

"Did you argue before she left?" Gareth asked.

Victoria snorted a laugh. "Argue? Holly? She could have been absolutely furious with me, and she would never say a word."

"Would you have known if she were absolutely furious with you?" Gareth picked up a spoon and stirred his tea.

Victoria considered the question. Her kneejerk reaction was to answer yes. But the truth was that she probably wouldn't. What did she care if her assistant was upset by something?

"I'm not sure why I would care," Victoria said.

She reached over, grabbed a cup and saucer, and put them in front of her. With a swirl of the teapot she poured herself a cup of the dark liquid.

"I can't tell the judge that you frequently drive staff to up and quit, that you just assumed Holly had done the same. That you don't particularly care about your staff and then say that you request power of attorney over someone who left your employment after what you yourself refer to as a tense week."

Victoria bristled at the implication.

"What do you recommend?" she asked.

"Did you and Holly have a different relationship to that

of your previous assistants? Could we explain why you are willing to take this responsibility on?"

"What are you implying?" she asked coldly.

Gareth laughed. "Nothing like that. Just, did you… mentor her? Were you closer because of… I don't know… a shared love of jazz? Anything?"

Victoria shrugged. "She walked my dog a couple of times. But then so has Louise."

"Louise?"

"My first assistant. I suppose I did feel closer to Holly, she was extremely good at her job." She picked up her cup to take a sip.

"Did you socialise?"

Victoria choked a little. She lowered her cup and dabbed her lip with the linen napkin.

"Socialise? No, of course not. She was my second assistant."

Gareth put down his spoon and lifted his cup. He drank the entire cup of tea in three large gulps. He put the cup back in the saucer and pushed it to one side.

"May I ask why you are doing this? Why do you want power of attorney over Holly? There are alternatives, she could be placed under state care, she—"

"She is coming home with me," Victoria said firmly.

"But why? You talk as if she was nothing to do with you, other than a good assistant. The only thing that you can think of that proves her being close is that she walked your dog a couple of times. You seem to have no tie to this girl, and yet you're about to spend a huge amount of time, money, and effort in caring for her. Why?"

"Because I have the time, the money, and I can spare

the effort to do so. She's an exceptional young girl who slipped through the cracks; she clearly has no family and when she joined *Arrival we* became her family. Holly Carter is a selfless, intelligent, caring human being who didn't deserve to spend a year of her life thinking that she was forgettable. She was anything but forgettable. I may not be the best person for the job, but I will do my damned utmost to ensure that she has the very best treatment. I will make sure she gets back on her feet and can live the rest of her life to the absolute fullest. I lost her once, I won't do it again."

Victoria stopped to take a breath. She held back a gasp at her own outburst. She had no idea where it had come from. Her cheeks started to heat.

"I think I can work with that," Gareth said. He picked up a stack of papers. "These papers are from the hospital, and they relate to Holly's treatment to date. It's probably a good idea for you to familiarise yourself with some of the history, in case the judge asks."

She took the papers, thankful for the distraction. *Tired and stressed*, she told herself. *Just tired and stressed.*

CHAPTER TWELVE

It was six o'clock in the evening when Victoria returned to the hospital. She marched up to the reception desk and whisked off her sunglasses.

"Holly Carter, *s'il vous plaît*."

The receptionist nodded and started typing on her computer before frowning, "Carter? C-A-R-T-E-R?"

Victoria sighed. "She may be listed as Clémence Dubois…"

"Ah, oui." The receptionist smiled. "You are the lady who has come to take Clémence home?"

"Holly. Carter." She was losing her patience with the whole Clémence Dubois scenario.

"Of course." The receptionist ducked her head. "I will call Doctor Fontaine for you. Please, take a seat." She gestured to a row of plastic chairs lined up against the wall.

Victoria slowly turned to look at the chairs. She sniffed disdainfully and stood tall, refusing to move. She couldn't recall the last time she had been asked to wait in a reception area. And certainly not in plastic chairs.

The receptionist made a telephone call, and within a few moments Charlotte Fontaine arrived.

"Bonsoir, welcome back."

"Merci." Victoria nodded.

"I see your legal team have been working hard. Our legal manager told me that everything seems to be ready for Holly's departure tomorrow."

"Indeed." Victoria offered a tight smile.

The last time she had been at the hospital she had felt off balance. The shock of seeing Holly again, the fear that she could be barred from seeing her in the future. Now she felt more like herself, more confident. She had an expensive lawyer behind her, and soon she wouldn't have to kowtow to the hospital staff.

"I also had a call from the NewYork-Presbyterian Hospital. Once the judge approves everything, I shall forward Holly's medical details to them," Charlotte said.

"Wonderful," Victoria said without feeling. She was very much aware that they were still standing in reception.

"I'm afraid Holly is unwell at present," Charlotte admitted. "Nothing too serious, but she does have a migraine. It is common with her type of brain injury, and I think all of the excitement today has caused it."

Victoria frequently suffered with tension headaches and migraines and felt a sliver of sympathy for Holly.

"Shall I come back tomorrow?" she asked.

Charlotte chuckled. "Oh, no, no. She would be furious with me if I let you leave without at least saying hello. She is in her room. Please, follow me."

Charlotte indicated the elevator with her hand. They

walked over, and Charlotte pressed the button to call the cart.

"She needs to lie down and take things slowly until the migraine passes, but I know she is eager to speak to you. I believe she has many more questions."

"I feared she might," Victoria mumbled.

"*Problème?*" Charlotte asked.

The elevator doors opened, and both women stepped in. Charlotte selected the correct floor.

"Holly only worked with me for under a year," Victoria explained. "And we were not, in anyway, close. Quite simply, I know hardly anything about her."

Charlotte nodded. "From my experience, you will know a lot more than you think. For example, someone with memory loss may ask if they have siblings, and we may be able to say, oui, you have a brother. But until a patient can connect with that fact on an emotional level, it will only be a statement and not a feeling.

"You may not have the facts and figures, but maybe you can provide something better? A description of how she has a messy desk? An observation that she hates early mornings? How she sings when she files documents away? Maybe these real-life observations will help more than the cold, hard facts."

Victoria hadn't considered that. Maybe she did have worthwhile information to offer Holly. She could use her eye for detail to explain what Holly was like as a person rather than a list of vital statistics about her life.

The elevator gently bounced to a stop, and the doors opened.

Charlotte led the way down the corridors.

"What Holly needs most is love and care," she said.

Victoria nearly laughed out loud at the thought. Charlotte turned to face her, and Victoria offered an unsure and mildly terrified smile.

They stopped outside a wooden door that looked like it hadn't seen a fresh coat of paint since the eighties. Charlotte held up her hand for Victoria to wait a moment. She softly knocked on the door and opened it a crack.

"Holly, are you well enough to see Victoria?"

She heard a soft mumble from inside the room, and Charlotte gestured for Victoria to enter.

"I'll return later," she promised.

Charlotte backed out and closed the door behind her as Victoria hesitantly entered the small room.

She squinted in the dim light. The window was covered by shabby curtains to keep the glare of the lamppost out. The lodgings seemed more like a prison cell than a hospital room. She'd seen some of the wards earlier that day, they were large, shared spaces. She assumed that Holly had been assigned a room of her own due to the amount of time she had spent in the facility.

But the room was dated to say the least.

While the downstairs looked like a modern building, here they appeared to travel back in time. There was a sink, Victorian in style, and a shelf with a paltry selection of toiletries.

Beside the sink was a small, wooden writing desk with a few tatty books lined up neatly on the top. An old schoolhouse chair was tucked underneath. A rickety chest of drawers and a bed were the only other pieces of furniture in the dreary little room.

Her examination of the room complete, Victoria had no choice but to look at Holly who was laying on the bed. Holly was smiling, though her eyes were tear-filled. The contradiction made Victoria's heart ache.

"Excuse me if I don't get up," Holly whispered slowly.

"I'd be angry if you did." Victoria placed her handbag and coat on the small desk. She picked up the chair, gently placed it beside the bed, and sat down. "I hear today has been a little much for you?"

It was surreal to see Holly in pieces. The girl had always been so well put together, never showing Victoria weakness no matter how bad things got.

"Yeah," Holly admitted. "It has been quite a big day."

Victoria smiled. "If you want some peace and quiet, I could—"

"No." Holly raised her voice and started to sit up. Quickly she thought better of it, though. She closed her eyes and lowered herself down again. "No, I'd prefer it if you stayed. For a while, at least."

Victoria nodded and sat quietly, not sure what to do next.

"Have you changed your mind?" Holly whispered.

"About?"

"About taking on a brain-damaged wreck. I'm sure you have a life of your own…"

"Well, if you're going to be this depressing, then yes, I might leave you here," Victoria quipped. She picked a piece of lint from her skirt.

"You changed clothes," Holly pointed out.

"Yes, I was in a travelling outfit. When it became clear I wouldn't be travelling, I changed."

Holly chuckled softly.

"Is that amusing?" Victoria asked. She looked up to meet Holly's eyes.

"Yes," Holly said honestly. "I didn't know people had travelling outfits."

"Well, I do."

"I can't remember flying; do I like flying?" Holly asked.

Victoria had no idea. She thought back to the journey to Paris. Holly had been efficient as usual. She searched her memory further, trying to pick up on nuances that she wouldn't have cared about before. She recalled Holly gripping the armrests during take-off. But then many people did that.

If she were afraid of flying, Victoria would have been the last person she would have told.

"You never spoke of a fear of flying," she replied honestly.

"Good," Holly replied. "Do you… do you know when I might be able to leave?"

Victoria blinked. Suddenly she realised how out of the loop Holly was. A hive of activity was happening around her, but no one had properly spoken to her and given her the details of what had been decided. That was going to change.

"Actually, yes," she said. "My lawyers have managed to get us an appointment with the judge tomorrow morning. You and I will have to attend court, and you will have to answer some questions about your understanding of my having power of attorney. My lawyer will go through these questions with you before we go to the courtroom. Once that is done, you will be discharged from the hospital and into my care."

Despite the painful migraine, Holly's face held an ever-widening smile.

"Then we will have to go to the American Embassy," Victoria continued, "so that you can have your photograph taken for your new passport. That will be issued within the hour, and then we will be going straight to the airport and onto New York."

She noticed a small tear falling down Holly's cheek. Suddenly another, and then another joined it. She stood up and sat on the edge of the bed. She gently stroked the girl's short brown hair.

"Holly? What is it? What's wrong?"

"I'm happy," Holly said. "I'm not sad, don't worry."

Victoria smiled down at her and nodded. Using her thumb, she wiped the tears from Holly's cheeks.

"I just can't believe that after all this time, someone finally found me. And I'm going home," Holly whispered.

Victoria withdrew her hand and clasped it in her lap.

"I'd given up hope," Holly continued. "I thought I'd be thrown around in the French legal and medical systems for a few years before being kicked out. Then I'd be stuck in France, not knowing anyone. Not being able to communicate. Sure, I know some French, but they always talk to me in English, trying to jog my memory.

"And then you turned up. And now I'm going home. Even though I don't know anything about it, I don't have a clue what is coming next, I feel… I feel… whole. More… like myself. Like I'm finally getting somewhere. Finally, I'm on a journey back to being me. And I can't thank you enough. I promise you that I will pay you back for everything you have done for me, I don't know how, but I know that I will, somehow."

"Shh," Victoria soothed. "You don't need to pay me back. You don't need to worry about such things."

"It feels like this is all a dream, and I'm going to wake up."

"I assure you that this isn't a dream. However, you do need to rest." Victoria placed her hand on Holly's upper arm and squeezed gently through the sweater sleeve. "You need to be at your best for court tomorrow."

Holly nodded. "You'll be back tomorrow?"

"Of course, at nine o'clock." She stood up and replaced the chair under the desk. She picked up her coat and bag and stood in front of the bed. "Get some rest. Some sleep will do you good."

"Thank you. I'm sorry I haven't been better company."

Victoria couldn't help but feel that she had somehow been let off the hook. If Holly had been fit and healthy, then she surely would have had a hundred questions to throw at her. Questions she couldn't answer. Awkward silences that may have caused Holly to become concerned.

"You've been fine. Rest. I'll see you in the morning," Victoria said.

"I'll get my travelling outfit ready," Holly teased.

Victoria chuckled. Holly had never been one for jokes when she had worked for her. She presumed that she was now seeing the real Holly, the one beyond the shy assistant. She wondered what other surprises lurked.

"You do that," she replied. "Good night."

"'Night," Holly mumbled.

Victoria paused for a moment, watching as Holly closed her eyes and started to allow sleep to take her. She shook her head, wondering why she was standing around. With a final sneer at the room, she took her leave.

CHAPTER THIRTEEN

THE NEXT MORNING, a nurse was waiting to escort Victoria to Holly's room. He remained stoically silent the whole journey and merely gestured to Holly's door before walking away. Something didn't seem right, but she didn't have time to think about it right now. She had a limited amount of time to get Holly to the courtroom.

She knocked and entered the room, the empty Louis Vuitton holdall that she had picked up the evening before in her hand.

"You!" Holly exclaimed. She sat at her desk, fire dancing in her eyes.

"Me?" Victoria questioned. She placed the empty holdall on the bed.

"You! There is no way that I am going anywhere with you!" Holly shouted. She jumped to her feet and swiped the holdall off the bed, throwing it towards Victoria.

Victoria caught the bag before it hit her face. She glowered at Holly, wondering what kind of insanity she'd walked into.

"We don't throw Louis Vuitton, Holly," she said in her coldest tone. "Now, would you mind enlightening me as to what the hell is going on?"

"You are what is going on." Holly pointed at her. "You are such a fraud."

Victoria opened her mouth to again ask what was happening, but Holly cut her off before she could.

"I looked you up! Thank god I did before I was stuck on a plane with you! Did you think that they don't have the Internet in backwards old France? Huh? Well, they do! *Ice Queen*, that's what they call you. And *the Dragon*. No one has a single nice word to say about you. I read article after article. They all say that you are a backstabbing, manipulative, cold-hearted witch who only cares about herself."

Victoria looked down at the floor, trying to keep a lid on her irritation.

"And you've been here, acting like you're my best friend," Holly continued. "Being nice and charming, but that's not you at all, is it?"

Victoria sucked in a quick breath.

"Not going to deny it then?" The triumph in Holly's tone was clear.

Victoria looked up, pinning Holly with a stare. "Are you finished?" she asked.

"For now," Holly said.

"Good. Then allow me to reply in regards to my denial. Am I going to deny that journalists, competitors, ex-employees, and even my ex-husband have called me the Ice Queen or the Dragon? No. Am I going to deny that the press enjoys printing tales of my difficult nature, my inability to hold down a personal relationship, and my struggle to be heard as a powerful woman in a male-dominated corporate environment? No. Have I been called backstabbing? Yes. Manipulative? Yes. I haven't seen cold-hearted in print, but I'd be happy to take your word for it."

She threw the bag onto the bed and took a step closer to Holly.

"I'm aloof. Difficult to be around. I don't suffer fools gladly, or indeed at all. I have exacting standards, and punish those who cannot reach them. *Arrival* is not some high school newspaper, it's a critically acclaimed, multinational magazine published in twenty-three countries every single month. I am the editor-in-chief of the American edition and every other editor around the world looks to me to set an example. *Arrival* is valued at more than three hundred and fifty million dollars and, with no word of exaggeration, that is because of me. I carry the company on my shoulders. So, no, I'm sorry, but I don't have the luxury of being a sweet, approachable best pal to the world and I make no apology for that.

"Am I the best person to care for you? Absolutely not. Do I wish you any harm? No. Will I do my best to ensure you are looked after and provided with everything you need to make a full and speedy recovery? You bet I will. I may be cold-hearted, but I am all you have at the moment. And, if you wish to go your own way once we reach New York, then you have my word that I will assist you in doing just that. I'll do my best to continue to maintain my nice and charming *act* as best I can, but now you'll know the truth of the dragon beneath the mask."

She hadn't raised her voice once. She'd maintained an

even tone, stood less than a metre away from Holly, and never let her gaze waver.

Holly stared at her for a long while, shock and horror clear on her face.

"I… I'm sorry. I don't know what came over me," Holly took a step back and fell into her chair. "I'm so sorry, I shouldn't have spoken to you like that."

"I think perhaps you're remembering me and who I am." Victoria sniffed and took a step back.

"No, not at all. You're a complete mystery to me, I don't remember a thing," Holly confessed. "I think that's why I went off the deep end like that. I thought that you were tricking me somehow. I'm sorry, I shouldn't have said those things. Of course, the fashion world must be very cutthroat, people will say things like that. There's bound to be gossip. Especially about someone like you."

Victoria cocked her head to the side. "Well, some of it may be gossip, but most of it is rather accurate…"

Holly licked her chapped lips nervously. "You should leave me here," she said. "I think this is probably just an indication of how much trouble I'm going to cause you."

Victoria nodded. "True, but I'm sure you'll be much more trouble as time progresses. Just as you were before." She offered a small smirk to Holly to show that she was joking.

Holly grinned. "That bad, huh?"

"Utterly abysmal, you wouldn't believe how long it took you to get coffee," Victoria deadpanned.

She picked up the holdall and held it towards Holly.

"Now, pack your bag with whatever you're bringing, and meet me in reception in five minutes."

"Are you sure?" Holly asked.

"Are you?" Victoria returned.

Holly looked at the holdall and then up at Victoria. She quickly nodded her head. "Yes, I'm sure."

"Then so am I. Five minutes, Holly." Victoria spun on her heel and left the room.

Victoria paced the reception area. Her mind was running wild following the confrontation with Holly. She knew about the countless articles online that spoke ill of her. Some of them were fabricated, but many of them were accurate. In a way, she enjoyed the notoriety. Having people quake in their Louboutins wasn't a bad thing when you were making outrageous demands.

Of course, she'd had long conversations with her children about the lies they may uncover online. And even sometimes when the articles weren't lies. Having work acquaintances think she was a monster was one thing, her son and her daughter were another matter entirely.

Explaining herself wasn't something she did often, but when she did, it was to a loved one. To her children, her parents, her husband… now ex-husband. And now she found herself doing the same for Holly. Extenuating circumstances, she reminded herself.

"Victoria," Charlotte Fontaine caught her attention and stood beside her to prevent her pacing.

Victoria stopped her patrol and nodded her greeting to the doctor.

"I have just spoken with Holly," Charlotte explained. "She is very upset about her outburst."

"It's water under the bridge." Victoria waved her hand to end the conversation.

Charlotte frowned, clearly not understanding the expression.

"We discussed it, and we agreed to move on," Victoria corrected.

"Good, I'm very pleased to hear that," Charlotte said. "Would you say that Holly's behaviour was usual for her?"

Victoria shook her head. "No, Holly would never have spoken to me like that."

Charlotte nodded. "Interesting. We've never experienced an outburst like that from Holly. As we have no benchmark, it is difficult for us to tell if her behaviour is normal, stress-related, or from damage to her frontal lobe."

Victoria considered the statement for a moment. Holly would never have dared to have spoken like that to her face. But behind her back, Victoria wouldn't have blamed her one bit.

"I hope it is simply stress," Victoria noted.

"Agreed. As I say, we have never seen that kind of outburst before, so it is most likely that it was stress. But if it was something more, I'm sure her American doctors will pick up on it."

"They will," Victoria agreed. She'd called her contacts and found the best doctors in New York. They were standing by and ready to receive Holly's medical reports.

Holly walked into reception in a pair of skinny black jeans with a casual white t-shirt and a fashionably ripped pale blue sweater over the top. She held her newly acquired, and apparently sparsely filled, holdall loosely by her side.

She looked nervous, wide eyes flitting around the reception area like a child on her first day of school.

A nurse walked into reception and swept her into a hug. Before long there were more nurses pouring into the small reception area to wish her farewell. Small gifts and cards were handed over. Holly had tears in her eyes, and she hugged them all goodbye.

One of the nurses took the holdall from her and placed the presents and envelopes inside. Holly made her way to Charlotte, who also pulled her into an embrace.

"Holly, it has been a real pleasure getting to know you," Charlotte said. "You must take good care of yourself. I want you to stay in touch and tell me everything about New York, oui?"

The pair parted but held hands.

"Oui, I will write to you as soon as I can," Holly promised.

A nurse held out Holly's holdall for her. She took it, offering a huge smile of gratitude as she did.

"We need to go," Victoria prompted. She wanted to get away from the claustrophobic overflow of emotions.

Holly nodded. She turned around, waved, and said a final farewell. Victoria was already retreating down the steps and towards the waiting limousine, knowing that Holly would follow her.

Things were returning to normal.

CHAPTER FOURTEEN

Victoria folded her arms and stepped between Holly and Gareth, glaring at Gareth as she did so.

"You're scaring her half to death," the formidable woman complained.

"I'm okay," Holly mumbled, trying to get Victoria's attention.

Gareth, Victoria's English lawyer, held up his hands to calm her. He looked around Victoria to meet Holly's eyes.

"Sorry, Miss Carter. I don't mean to frighten you, but I do need to prepare you for the questions the judge is going to ask."

Holly nodded. "It's okay. I understand."

Victoria stepped back again. Holly had been surprised at how quickly she had leapt to her defence. Gareth had been explaining the process, and Holly could feel the stress building within her. It had clearly manifested itself on her face, and Victoria had seen and taken action. It was a nice feeling to have someone so powerful on her side.

They were in the opulent waiting room of the courthouse. The marble floor and high ceilings caused their words to echo softly around the empty room. Oil paintings hung on the walls, and busts of important looking men looked at her with stony scowls.

Gareth looked at Victoria. "Remember that you need to remain absolutely silent until spoken to when we get in there."

Victoria's glare could have melted steel. Holly was relieved that she wasn't on the receiving end of it.

Gareth didn't seem fazed. "I've done some research on the judge, and he is extremely strict. He won't like an American woman coming in and telling him how to run his courtroom. The quickest and most efficient way of getting out of here is speaking when spoken to, saying as little as possible, and most of all, sticking to the script."

Victoria maintained her fiery stare for a few moments more. Finally, she rolled her eyes and, with a slight nod of her head, agreed.

Gareth turned back to Holly. His face softened. "Are you ready to continue the questions? I'd like for you to be as prepared as possible."

"Absolutely, fire away," Holly said.

She was keen to hear what Gareth had to say. The whole court process was terrifying to her. The very idea that someone who had never met her would be making a decision about her well-being was baffling. The fear that he would disagree with what Victoria had in mind was causing Holly's heart to beat like a drum.

Gareth gestured towards one of the wooden benches against the wall, and Holly followed him. Victoria remained standing, glancing up at the golden clock high on the wall.

In the short amount of time she'd known Victoria, Holly had discovered that time was a very important concept for her. Victoria hated the idea of being late, and her own clock seemed to run a few minutes ahead of everyone else's. A ten o'clock meeting should start at nine fifty-five. Holly made a mental note of the fact.

"Okay," Gareth began.

She pulled her attention away from Victoria and towards Gareth. She tried to fully focus on him, despite her nerves.

"Let's go through the process one last time," he suggested.

Holly nodded and took a deep breath. She needed to focus. Today could be the first day of the rest of her life.

CHAPTER FIFTEEN

Exactly one hour later, Holly walked down the steps of the courthouse clutching a piece of paper and smiling more than she could ever remember.

Gareth was right beside her. Holly indicated the signed and stamped power of attorney and then pointed to Victoria.

"Does this mean she owns me now?" she joked.

"Yes," Gareth confirmed with a grin. "Until such time that she exchanges you for livestock."

Holly giggled.

Victoria sniffed. "You two are utterly ridiculous." She brushed past them and continued down the steps towards the waiting limousine.

Holly knew she didn't mean it. She'd looked at Victoria when the judge had approved the power of attorney and noticed the stern woman smiling. Of course, the smile quickly vanished, and a knowing nod of the head replaced it when she realised Holly was looking at her.

Gareth softly put his hand on her shoulder. She turned to look at him, and he handed her his business card.

"Call me if you need anything, like if you need the power of attorney dissolved. I'll get it arranged for you," he said, a tip of the head towards Victoria as he spoke.

Holly took the card. "I think I'll be fine," she said. "I think her bark is a lot worse than her bite."

He grinned. "I think so, too. But, just in case, eh?"

She pocketed the business card. "Thank you, I really appreciate all you've done."

"We're not done yet," he said. "Next stop, the embassy. We need to get you that passport or you'll miss your flight."

Victoria was already in the car, probably sighing and periodically glaring at her watch in annoyance. Gareth was the next in and Holly quickly followed him. The driver closed the door behind her.

She'd been so nervous on the way to the courthouse that she'd hardly noticed the journey. Now she felt like she was in safe hands. The judge had granted her power of attorney and that effectively released her into Victoria's care. And Victoria didn't seem like the kind of woman who didn't get exactly what she wanted when she wanted it. They were due to fly to New York in under five hours, and Holly was certain that would be the case.

She was aware that Gareth and Victoria were talking, but Holly tuned them out. She looked out of the window at the imposing courthouse and wondered if she'd ever see Paris again. Paris had been her home for the past year, or for as long as she could remember, but it had never felt truly like home. Knowing that she was American made her ache to be there, even if she had no recollection of what it was like.

Part of her treatment had been to watch American television shows and movies to see if she recognised anything. She didn't, but it did build an overwhelming desire to see the country that she called home.

Now she was on her way. The butterflies fluttered in her stomach, and she closed her eyes momentarily. She was on her way to discovering the truth about herself and her life.

CHAPTER SIXTEEN

The airport was enormous and filled with people rushing around. Holly struggled with the noise and the pace of activity. It was quite different from her quiet hospital. She wondered how she would cope with the busy streets of New York if she was already halfway to a panic attack in the airport.

Luckily, she had Victoria. And with Victoria came first-class everything, including a private lounge within which to eat a meal before the flight.

The moment they stepped through the doors and breezed past reception, she let out a sigh of relief. A waiter almost fell over himself to seat them at the best table in the lounge. Holly was starting to understand just how big of a deal Victoria was.

They had both ordered, and Victoria had quickly started to work. She placed an iPad Mini on a stand on the table and scrolled through her emails. At the same time, she spoke to various people on her phone. Before the food arrived, Holly had heard Victoria speaking in at least three different languages.

She wondered if she herself had known any languages. She spent a lot of time wondering about her previous self. There was so little else to occupy her in the hospital. All her treatments revolved around trying to help her to remember her past life, so it was impossible to escape the enormous question mark that had been her life prior to the accident.

The accident had hit the reset button on her brain. And in some ways, she was about to do the same again. She was about to leave everything and everyone she knew. She was now in the care of some almighty fashion guru who wore specific travelling outfits. She was about to fly for nine hours to her home country, which she had no memory of.

"Aren't you hungry?" Victoria questioned, her eyes transfixed on Holly's mainly uneaten meal. "Or is something wrong with your food? Would you like something else?"

Victoria was already turning around to seek out the waiter.

"No, no," Holly yelped to reclaim her attention. "It's wonderful, I'm just not very hungry. I'm a bit nervous."

"About the flight? You'll be fine. You get used to it soon enough." Victoria waved her hand dismissively and returned her attention to her iPad.

"I don't think it's the flight I'm nervous about," Holly admitted. "More… everything."

Victoria looked at her over the rim of her glasses. She scrutinised Holly for a few moments.

"You should try to take your mind off things," she said.

"Easier said than done," Holly replied.

Holly lifted her fork and started to pick at her food, hoping it may soothe her queasy stomach.

"Why don't you read? I noticed that your bag contains practically nothing but books."

Holly chuckled. "Yeah, they're all my worldly possessions. When I first started to recover, I couldn't read very well, so I practiced a lot and found out that I really enjoy it. But there weren't very many English books around, so the ones I have are old and donated by the staff at the hospital. I've probably read each one thirty times or more. Some aren't even stories."

She reached down to the bag and unzipped it. She pulled the first dilapidated book out and placed it on the table. "This one is about clouds, mainly. Sometimes it goes into the possible theory of a god sitting on a cloud. But mainly, it's clouds all the way."

She reached into the bag, pulled out another book, and put it on the table.

"This one, well, this beauty is about train stations in Moscow. Which I'm afraid to say is actually quite interesting. The first time. But when you have little to do and you have read it several times—"

"Please get those off the table." Victoria turned her nose up.

Holly put the books back in her bag. When she sat upright again, Victoria had pulled her iPad in front of her and was swiping away at the screen.

"What books do you like reading?" Victoria asked.

"Oh, I like everything," Holly replied. "I think I like the classics the best. I have two books by Charles Dickens that I like a lot. I have a more modern book about some career woman's romance, but that's not really my sort of thing, I don't think."

Victoria nodded. "Crime? History? Humour? Science fiction?"

"Um. I guess?" Holly answered. "Not sure about crime, I haven't really read any. History, yes. Did I mention the three whole chapters on the Moscow train stations during the forties? Humour, yes. I'm not sure about science fiction. Never read any."

As Holly spoke, Victoria tapped away on her iPad. She sat up and nodded with satisfaction and handed the device to Holly.

Holly hesitantly took it and frowned.

"I've bought the current top one hundred books according to the *New York Times*. They are downloading. I'm sure you'll find something that suits you there."

Holly gasped and looked at the iPad as if it were made of gold. She knew that this was too much, especially on top of everything else that Victoria was giving her. She handed the device back to Victoria.

"That's very generous, but I can't take this. You need it to do your work."

"Nonsense, I have my laptop. And I'll probably rest on the journey anyway." Victoria gestured for the waiter to take her plate.

Holly placed the device beside her own plate. "Then I'll gratefully accept it. Thank you."

"You're welcome." Victoria took a sip of water.

Holly looked at the iPad with interest. "How do you use it?"

Victoria looked startled. "Oh, well, it's rather easy. In fact, you taught me."

Holly laughed. "Did I? Wow."

"Yes, I was rather late on the party when it came to tablets and such. You installed all the applications and synched it with my laptop." Victoria almost looked wistful as she recalled the memory.

As quickly as that look had come over her, it vanished again. She shook her head, removed the napkin from her lap, and placed it on the table. She shuffled her chair closer to Holly and looked at the iPad.

"As I said, it's all rather simple…"

CHAPTER SEVENTEEN

Victoria gestured for Holly to walk in front of her. She placed her hand gently on the girl's back and guided her towards the airbridge.

She normally wouldn't be considered a tactile person, but for some reason Holly was bringing out another side of her. At the embassy, she'd quickly stood between Holly and the buffoon with the camera. Her fingers deftly brushed through Holly's short locks before her brain had engaged and she'd stepped back.

At the time, she had made the point that a passport photograph was something Holly would have to live with for a few years and pressed that it was important to look one's best. But the truth was that she'd acted without thinking.

Just a short time before, she'd been sitting shoulder to shoulder with Holly as they looked at the iPad. Their hands touched occasionally as they skimmed over the iPad screen, pointing to icons and swiping. She'd never touched Holly before, but now it was becoming a habit.

A habit that she needed to break.

Holly stopped dead in the middle of the airbridge. Victoria nearly walked into her.

"No way," Holly said firmly. She pointed towards the window. "No way can that thing fly. Look at it."

Victoria looked through the window to the Boeing 757 that they were on their way to board.

"Don't be absurd. Of course it can fly. If it couldn't fly, then how did it get here?"

"Look at it, it must weigh a million tonnes," Holly whispered through clenched teeth.

Victoria noted the other first-class passengers starting to walk around them.

"Why don't you focus your attention on those colossal ten-million-dollar apiece engines that are designed to carry the enormously over-exaggerated weight of the aircraft?" Victoria replied.

Holly spun around and glared at Victoria. "You said I wasn't afraid of flying!"

"You never told me that you were," Victoria argued.

"Well, let me show you something." Holly drew an imaginary ring around her face with her index finger. "This, this is me… afraid of flying."

"Very mature." Victoria sighed. She lowered her sunglasses from the top of her head, aware of the scene they were creating. "It's not even that big. If we were flying from London, it would hold another three hundred passengers. It would have another floor."

Holly looked incredulous. "So, we're on a smaller plane and we're travelling farther? Thank you for not helping."

Victoria rolled her eyes in exasperation. She took a step forward and put her hand soothingly on Holly's shoulder.

"I promise you that it is safe. Hundreds of thousands of these aircraft fly all across the world every year without incident. Yes, it's noisy. And, yes, it's daunting, but I swear to you that it is perfectly safe."

Holly looked into her eyes, or at least at her own reflection in Victoria's sunglasses.

"Take a deep breath in," Victoria instructed slowly. "And then another one out."

Holly did as she was instructed.

"Now, we're going to get on the plane and we're going to take our seats. I promise you that you will hate take-off. But once we are up in the air, you will wonder what all the fuss was about. You'll look back at this and laugh."

Holly slowly nodded. Victoria squeezed her shoulder and then let go. She gestured for Holly to walk in front of her.

"If we die, I will never let you hear the end of it," Holly mumbled as she walked towards the aircraft door.

As predicted, the take-off had been horrendous. Holly had gritted her teeth and held the armrests in a vicelike grip.

Victoria had no idea how to comfort her, so she had left her to her panic. Instead, she flicked through the inflight magazine with a critical eye and a sneer. Despite her attention being focused on the magazine, she was very much aware of what was happening next to her. She wondered if offering Holly the much desired window seat was such a good idea. Out of the corner of her eye she had seen the girl flipping between staring in awe and tightly closing her eyes.

It wasn't long before she started to feel a headache creeping at her temples. She had forgotten how exhausting it was to look after someone else. Hugo was fifteen and practically an adult in his own mind. Alexia was eight going on fifty. Then again, she'd always employed the services of a nanny from the moment her children were born.

Watching over Holly was like having a second full-time job.

Once take-off was over and Holly had released her death grip on the innocent armrests, Victoria leaned her head into the leather headrest and closed her eyes.

Victoria was no expert when it came to the art of sleeping. She spent her entire life in a state of hyperawareness. Even with her eyes closed, she was completely aware of her surroundings. The rumble of the cabin crew trolley, the chuckling of someone watching an inflight movie. And, of course, the woman sitting next to her.

It would be fair to say that Holly wore her heart on her sleeve, but knowledge of that fact didn't stop Victoria being surprised at her ability to monitor Holly's emotions, even with her eyes shut.

She could sense the girl's fears slowly fade. After a while, she heard a pen scratching its way over the scrappy notebook the girl seemed so fond of. She could practically feel excitement emanating from the girl.

Victoria had been lying with her eyes closed for around fifty minutes, but it had seemed like hours. It was clear that sleep wasn't going to come and whisk her away. She was far too curious about what Holly was up to. She opened her eyes and tilted her head towards her neighbour.

"Out with it," she muttered.

"Oh! You're awake!" Holly beamed. "I've been making plans." She folded printed pieces of paper up and slid them back into her notebook.

"I know," Victoria sighed.

"Sorry, did I keep you awake?"

Victoria waved the question away. "No, no… just tell me what you've been doing."

"Well," Holly started excitedly, "I think I've finally chosen a hostel. I had three to pick from. One is a good backup in case the first one is closed or not what I was expecting—"

"Hostel?" Victoria questioned with distaste. "You mean hotel? Why would you need a hotel?"

"I don't, I need a hostel," Holly corrected her. "You know, somewhere to live. My apartment will be long gone, even if I knew where it was. So, for now, I'll get a hostel until I can find a job and get a few months' pay. Then I can try to rent a room in a house…" Holly drifted off as Victoria stared at her.

"You will not be staying in a… *hostel*," Victoria almost spat the word. "You will, of course, be staying with me."

"I can't stay with you forever, Victoria. It's not right. I already owe you so much. No, the sooner I'm independent and out from under your feet, the better," Holly said triumphantly, her accompanying nod seemingly agreeing the matter for both parties.

"Who said forever?" Victoria pinched the bridge of her nose to relieve some of the stress that was building.

Holly rolled her eyes. "Whatever. Once we land, I'd like to go to this hostel to have a look around. I have the emergency funds they gave me at the embassy. It will depend on their availability, of course, but I hope I can get settled immediately. And then I won't be such a bother to you." Holly circled the address in her notebook.

Victoria picked up the tatty book and peered at the addresses. To say the addresses were located on the wrong side of town would be an understatement.

"Absolutely not." She tossed the book back to Holly. "I forbid it."

Holly's mouth fell open. "Excuse me? You what?"

It felt like the cabin temperature dropped by five degrees.

Victoria sighed and started again. "I'm sorry, I didn't mean to say that. It's just that it... it will be late when we get back to the city. And I don't want you, or me, to be lost in one of those neighbourhoods late at night looking for a hostel when I have a perfectly good guestroom for you to stay in."

Holly looked like she was going to argue.

"At least for tonight," Victoria hurriedly added. "Of course, you are welcome to stay as long as you like. But at least tonight, maybe the next as well, until you settle a little. We have so much to do, speak with your doctors, find your old apartment, locate your friends, find your bank account... so much to do. It would be better for you to remain at the townhouse. At least for the first week."

Victoria wanted more. She wanted Holly to stay for the first six months, maybe even a year. After spending so much time without her, it now felt imperative that she have Holly close. If only to ensure that she was safe and well. The thought of her living out of sight in New York was too much to bear. How would she know if Holly was safe if she were out of sight?

Holly still had a face like thunder but appeared to be taking the words into consideration.

"Fine." She nodded. "But as soon as the administrative stuff is done, I will go to the hostel."

Victoria rolled her eyes. "Why a hostel?"

"Because they're cheap. I'm unemployed and I need to get back on my feet again. I can't afford a New York hotel."

She frowned. "You're not unemployed."

Holly frowned in return. "Yes, I am."

"You work for me, you're my second assistant. I told you all of this."

Holly looked incredulous. "I *was* your second assistant, a year ago. I'm sure you've replaced me by now, and even if you haven't, I can't do that job now. I know nothing about it. I'd be no help to you at all. No, I need to start over. I need a new job, a new home. A new me."

Victoria headache spiked. She massaged her temple.

"You seem intent on causing me pain and removing yourself from my presence as soon as humanly possible," she mumbled.

"That's not true," Holly said softly. "I'm sorry your head hurts, and I'm sorry you can't sleep. But I want to get back on my feet as soon as possible. I haven't been able to do anything for myself for a year. Before that, I can't even remember. I want to be independent. I'm not trying to *hurt* you, I'm trying to help *me*."

"I'm trying to help you, too," Victoria whispered.

"I know," Holly admitted. "And I can't tell you how much I appreciate everything you are doing. I know you want to protect me and look after me, but I need to do some things for myself... I don't need you mothering me."

Victoria turned away and stared at the back of the seat in front of her.

Holly gently placed her hand on hers. "Do you understand what I'm saying?"

Victoria gave a small nod and closed her eyes.

CHAPTER EIGHTEEN

AFTER THE ARGUMENT, Holly had spent her time reading on the iPad. No matter how much she tried to bury herself in her book, she couldn't forget the altercation. She was split between feeling angry at Victoria's bossy behaviour and guilty at causing her pain. Victoria had seemed genuinely upset that Holly wanted to leave her so soon.

Holly wanted to talk about it, but Victoria's sudden silence and refusal to even look at her was a clear indication that the subject was closed. Soon after, Victoria had fallen asleep, or at least presented a good approximation of sleep.

The crew started to breeze through the cabin, issuing instructions at a blistering rate. There was talk of window blinds, chairs, hand luggage, restrooms, and tables, all at such a dizzying speed that Holly struggled to keep up.

She decided that the whole flying business was bonkers. Clearly the airline staff just enjoyed the buzz they received in bossing first-class passengers around.

During the flurry of activity, Victoria opened her eyes and looked around with a calculating glance. Holly watched as she pushed a button and returned her seat to an upright position. Then she pushed her handbag under the seat in front of her with a shoeless foot.

Holly hadn't reclined her seat and her luggage was in the overhead compartment, so she presumed that she was ready for the horror that was about to be the landing.

She itched to say something to Victoria. But after the hours of uneasy silence, she really didn't know what it was. She was so grateful for everything that Victoria was doing for her. Holly felt she needed to somehow pay her back, but what Victoria had given her was truly priceless. And now she wanted to give her more, a guestroom, a job, a life. Her old life. But Holly didn't remember that old life, she didn't even know if she wanted that life back.

"Seatbelt," Victoria whispered.

"Oh!" Holly glanced down at her lap and quickly pulled the belts together. "Thank you."

She sensed that Victoria wanted to say more. She was relieved that she wasn't the only one struggling with the way they had left things.

After a few more moments, Victoria spoke so softly that Holly could only just hear her.

"I'm sorry if you feel I am... *mothering* you... too much. I don't wish to lay down the law or use words like 'forbid.' It just happens because I worry. I don't want to see you hurt again. I feel I know best and I want to protect you from things, but I know that is wrong. I know you need to live your own life."

Holly got the distinct impression that Victoria didn't often apologise or admit fault.

"Thank you," Holly replied. "I can see you care for me a

lot, and I really do appreciate that. I think maybe I need to try to take my independence one step at a time. I think I have a tendency to leap in with both feet. We need to meet each other halfway…"

"Agreed."

Victoria looked relieved and her tensed shoulders slowly started to lower. They shared a smile.

It was short-lived, as the plane banked sharply. Holly pressed her back into the chair and grabbed hold of the armrests.

Why people continued to fly, she would never understand.

CHAPTER NINETEEN

Victoria had thought ahead and asked for a new driver from the agency. The last thing she needed was someone who would recognise Holly and cause a whirlwind of gossip in the office.

The second they exited the airport, Holly's nose was practically glued to the window, staring at the famous skyline before them. Victoria used the opportunity to get some work done.

She found herself distracted by Holly's occasional gasp at the scenery. After a while, she found her attention drifting towards the window that Holly was looking out of. She calculated the route they were taking and waited with a smile for Holly to be wowed by the view of Manhattan from the Robert Kennedy Bridge.

A small fear had lurked within Victoria, one which dreaded that Holly might dislike the grittiness of New York and prefer the beauty of Paris. That fear shrivelled up and vanished at the reflection of Holly's excited face.

The journey from the airport to the brownstone on

West 96th had never seemed shorter. The driver opened the front door and started to take the bags up the exterior flight of stairs and into the hallway.

Victoria climbed the stairs but suddenly felt a chill surround her. She'd expected Holly to be beside her, but the girl had vanished.

She whirled around only to let out a breath of relief when she saw Holly petting the neighbour's Persian cat. She exhaled the panic and inhaled a calming breath.

"Holly?" she called softly.

She wanted to get Holly into the safety of the house, as if the sanctuary of her own home would magically cleanse the fear and stress she had been suffering from.

Holly looked up at her and smiled.

"He's so cute," she said, gesturing her head to the cat.

"He is," Victoria agreed.

She hated the overly friendly, pretentious ball of fluff. The cat was one of the main reasons she'd bought a dog. A big dog.

Holly stood and walked up the stairs and into the house.

"Wow," she whispered in awe as she entered.

The driver had finished with the bags, and Victoria nodded her appreciation to him. He jogged back down the stairs and Victoria stepped into the house, closing the front door behind them and letting out a sigh. It was over. They were home. She'd done it.

She watched as Holly strolled around the entrance hall. She pressed her lips together in a worried, thin line. She'd been concerned about this moment as she wondered if

Holly would suddenly remember the house and her time inside it.

Holly had often been asked to deliver things to the house. Victoria imagined that the entrance hall had been a highly stressful location to the once shy girl.

Holly didn't seem to be experiencing a terrifying flashback. Instead she was staring at the high, ornately decorated ceilings and then shifting her gaze down to study the marble floor. She approached the long staircase to the right-hand side of the building, looking up and then down.

"Wow," she repeated. "You have a beautiful home."

"Quite the statement seeing as you've only seen the hallway," Victoria muttered. She felt a satisfied smile tug at her lips. She removed her coat and hung it in the closet.

"I'd happily live in the hallway," Holly replied.

"Well, luckily for you, you won't have to. A guestroom has been made up for you downstairs."

Holly looked over the bannister rail again. She turned her whole body around to look up. "How many floors are there?"

"Five. The guest area is downstairs, there's a bedroom, an en suite, and kitchen facilities. But I'd love for you to dine with the family, if you are agreeable?"

Holly removed herself from the bannister and nodded. "I'd prefer to. Where are your children?"

"With my mother, they'll be back next week."

"Have you… told them? About me, I mean?"

Victoria shook her head. "No, not yet. I'll speak with them before they return, though."

"Will they be okay with it?" Holly asked.

"I don't see why not. We've had guests come to stay before."

"But presumably not former second assistants who have brain damage?"

She didn't really have a reply to that, and she didn't really need one. She was Victoria Hastings, she did what she liked. If she were to be unpredictable, no one would call her out on it.

"Please do go down to your room. Unpack, freshen up, etcetera. I'm going to get changed and then I'll prepare us a small dinner if you like?"

"Thank you, that's very kind." Holly walked over to the stack of luggage and picked up her holdall.

"Not at all." She picked up the smallest of her four suitcases. "Shall we say thirty minutes?"

CHAPTER TWENTY

The holdall slipped from Holly's fingers and fell to the thick carpeted floor with a muted thud. She stared at her surroundings, her mouth hanging open in shock.

The so-called guestroom was out of this world. Immaculately decorated, homey and comforting. It had the feel of a boutique hotel, the soft tartan wallpaper matching the bedspread on the king-sized sleigh bed.

Two large sash windows drew light from the back yard, but an outside wall covered in ivy and lilac roses maintained a level of privacy.

Holly walked into the en suite bathroom, flipping the switch to activate the spotlights in the ceiling. The first thing she noticed was a shower big enough for six people, a series of water jets built into the wall and the ceiling made it look like an experience not to be missed. A shelf in the shower area was filled with shampoos, conditioners, body washes, and other products she couldn't recognise.

She turned to look at the bathtub and noticed more beauty products lined up along the edge. The sink and vanity area held wrapped toothbrushes, toothpaste, hairbrushes, and makeup.

Holly couldn't remember if she'd ever stayed in a luxury hotel, but she was pretty sure that no hotel was as luxurious as this.

She walked back into the bedroom and opened the nearest wardrobe. It was full of clothes, beautiful designer clothes. She pulled out a garment on a hanger and noted it was her size. Along the bottom of the wardrobe was a variety of shoes for all occasions. Again, in her size. She put the hanger back and closed the door of the wardrobe.

She turned and started to explore further. A set of drawers held a large selection of underwear. The bedside cabinet was full of stationery, including leather-bound notebooks and a selection of pens. The vanity unit contained face cleansers, moisturisers, and perfume.

She stood in the doorway to the bathroom and gaped at the two rooms in astonishment.

Victoria had taken care of absolutely everything. Anything Holly could need for the next month was available to her. It was obvious that great thought and care had gone into making the temporary stop a home. She felt touched at the thought of Victoria taking so much effort just for her.

She wondered if it was Victoria, or maybe her first or even her second assistant. But surely they would have had guidance from Victoria?

Holly picked up her holdall and placed it on the bench at the end of the bed. She opened the bag and took out her notebook and cheap ballpoint pen. She walked around the room a little, taking everything in for a few moments. Eventually, she sat on the corner of the bed and started to write.

At first, writing had been a training exercise, a way to improve her motor skills, but it had soon become a big part of her life. She enjoyed jotting down her thoughts and feelings, mentioning noteworthy moments about her day and reading back through days gone by. It became a way to process what she was going through.

She knew that today's entry would take a long time to properly document. Probably more pages than she had left in her book. But then there were the new leather-bound notebooks that had been supplied. Surely Victoria had played a part in that? That wasn't usual guestroom material, was it?

A smile broke out across her face, gaining in size and strength until it started to hurt her cheeks.

CHAPTER TWENTY-ONE

VICTORIA POURED some salt into the large pan of nearly boiling water. She stretched her shoulders and let out a sigh. It had been a very long day, no doubt one of many long days to come.

She could hear the distinctive sound of a lost soul walking around the ground floor of the house. A smile curled her lips.

"In here, Holly," she called out softly.

A few moments later, Holly appeared in the kitchen. "I'll need a map for this place. And I've only been on two of the floors!"

"You'll get used to it," Victoria told her.

Holly walked over to the kitchen island where the saucepan gently bubbled. She leaned on the countertop and looked at Victoria seriously. "Victoria, we have to talk. My room—"

"Is something wrong?" Victoria interrupted.

"No, nothing like that. It's beautiful. Amazing, even."

"Then?"

"It's too much," Holly said. "I appreciate everything you have done and are doing, but… there must be thousands of dollars of clothes, shoes, and toiletries down there."

Victoria gestured to Holly with the wooden spoon she had been holding. "You don't have many other clothes. And no toiletries to speak of."

Holly opened her mouth to respond, presumably to argue.

"Besides," Victoria continued, "it's just a few bits from the sample closet at *Arrival*. No one would use them anyway. They are at least a season old. The closet gets cleaned out once a year, so you've done the company a favour. I don't see the problem."

Holly smiled. "It's not a problem, I'm supremely grateful. I'm just finding it hard to accept all these generous gifts."

"They're not gifts," Victoria corrected. "They are necessities. Toothpaste and the like."

"And Hugo Boss perfume," Holly added with a chuckle.

"I believe it was your scent; I'd hoped it would jog your memory." Victoria angrily threw handfuls of pasta into the boiling pan of water. She felt foolish for admitting that she had taken the time to notice Holly's preferred mid-price scent.

Holly stared at her, disbelief on her face.

Victoria tried to ignore her but found that she couldn't.

"What?" she demanded.

"That's a wonderful thing to do, thank you. I'm sorry if I sounded ungrateful, but I'm not used to gifts. That you took the time and effort to find my usual perfume… wow."

As quickly as it had come, Victoria felt the anger wash

away. Holly wasn't teasing her. She was grateful. Her cheeks heated as a result.

"Yes, well, you're welcome." She gestured towards the saucepan. "I take it you like pasta?"

"I do," Holly confessed.

"Good, take a seat and it will be ready momentarily." Victoria pointed to the small family dining table. She'd decided against dinner in the large dining room, she felt the atmosphere wouldn't help Holly feel at home on her first night. Right now, the girl needed cosy, calm, and relaxing.

"Can I help with anything?" Holly asked.

Victoria looked up at her. She'd had an idea, something to make the evening special. But she wasn't sure if it was a good idea.

"Well, I know it's late and you're probably tired, but I was wondering if you'd like to open a bottle of wine to toast your homecoming?"

Holly's eyes lit up. "That sounds lovely. But I have to warn you that I haven't drunk alcohol for at least a year."

"Just one glass then," Victoria decided. "Could you get a couple of glasses from that cupboard by the window?"

Holly retrieved the glasses and placed them on the table. She hovered around helplessly for a few moments until Victoria told her to take a seat. Holly sat down, and Victoria quickly finished preparing the meal.

She placed two bowls of pasta on the table and went to the wine refrigerator to get an appropriate vintage.

"This looks delicious," Holly said, inhaling deeply above the bowl.

"Reserve your judgement until you've eaten it," Victoria warned. She opened and poured the wine. Then she sat down and held up her glass towards Holly. Holly raised her glass, too.

"Thank you," Holly said, before Victoria had a chance to speak. "To you, for bringing me home."

"No, no," Victoria argued. "To you, for being so extraordinarily brave despite all that you have been through."

Holly tilted her head to the side and shrugged.

They clinked glasses softly and sipped some of the sweet liquid.

"I'm not really that brave," Holly muttered as she lowered her glass and picked up her fork.

"I beg to disagree," Victoria replied. "You have been amazing throughout all of this ordeal. I don't think I would have handled the events of the last couple of days with the calm and grace that you have exhibited."

"If I've handled it with any calm or grace it's because of all the practice I've had during the last year. During my recovery, I quickly realised that the French are all about procedures and politics. I couldn't fight it, so I had to just not let it get to me." Holly took a bite of her food and hummed happily. "And this is just as delicious as it looks."

"Thank you. And, yes, you're right that the French are entirely process-driven and hierarchical. I'm surprised that *Arrival France* manages to get an edition out every month. But that does not take anything away from your remarkable composure. I fear I would have been very different if I had been in your shoes."

Holly laughed. "You'd never have been in my shoes. If you went missing for more than five minutes, then the army would be called in."

Victoria stared down at her meal and tossed a piece of

chicken in the pasta sauce. It was true, of course, but it wasn't easy to hear.

"Did I say something wrong?" Holly asked tentatively.

"No, no. I just… I struggle to think of you there for all that time. I should have checked that you got home safely. I should have… have… done something…"

"It's absolutely not your fault," Holly insisted.

Victoria looked up and meet sincere eyes.

"I walked away," Holly said. "What could you have done? No, whatever it was that happened, happened because of my actions and not yours. If I'd have stayed by your side, none of this would have happened, would it?"

Victoria didn't agree but knew it was pointless to argue. Instead she asked, "Do you remember anything at all about your past? Or the accident?"

Holly's brow furrowed. "It's hard to say. Sometimes I get a feeling that I remember something, but I don't really know. It's more like a sensation, a bit like déjà vu. But I don't remember anything from my accident, I don't know what happened to me at all. I just remember waking up in hospital and I couldn't understand what was happening… or what was being said…" Holly's look became distant.

Victoria decided that a change of subject was in order.

"We have an appointment tomorrow morning at Presbyterian with your new medical team, and then in the afternoon we are seeing my lawyer, Michael. He will assist in finding information on any bank accounts you may have, and any records of where you have lived. Hopefully we'll be able to piece together a few things that will bring back some memories."

"That's very generous of you, but I really can't take up

any more of your time. I know you need to get back to *Arrival*."

"Nonsense, I make my own schedule," Victoria sniffed.

"I know, but I don't want you to have to work ridiculous hours to catch up with anything you might have missed because you were with me," Holly said. "Really, I'll be fine. I can find my way around and deal with these things myself. I feel terrible for monopolising your time like this, and it would make me feel better to know that things are getting back to normal for you. I wouldn't feel like such a burden…"

Victoria's first instinct was to argue her point and tell Holly that she would be attending all appointments with her, no matter what. But she managed to stop herself and listen to what Holly was saying. Maybe it was a good idea to allow the girl some independence. She didn't want her to feel like she was a prisoner. She was free to do as she pleased, and it was important that she knew that.

"Very well," she agreed. "But the car will take you to your appointments. I don't want you to have to suffer the New York public transportation system just yet. And you must take my spare phone, so we can keep in touch if necessary."

Holly smiled broadly. "That sounds like a good compromise."

Victoria snorted a laugh. "Enjoy it while you can. You'll learn that I'm not good with compromise."

CHAPTER TWENTY-TWO

Gideon loved the design aesthetics of the *Arrival* offices. The modern feel, bright lights, and, most of all, the glass walls. The latter of which allowed him to see Victoria approaching his office.

He continued working, examining photographs, and leaning on his waist-high stand-up desk. When he heard the door open, he wordlessly pointed to a stool by the wall.

He heard Victoria sit down and then release a sigh.

He continued grouping the photographs for a few moments before he stood up straight, removed his glasses, and looked at her.

"The last time you came to see me, and sat on that chair, you were debating whether or not to ask James for a divorce after that whole mess…" He waved his hand around dismissively in lieu of finishing the sentence.

"Hm. And you gave me wonderful advice," she agreed.

"Always at your service." He folded his arms and leaned against the edge of the desk. "So, how is Holly? And more to the point, where is Holly?"

Victoria turned to regard the series of framed certificates and awards on the shelf by the window. "Staying with me, for the time being at least."

"Very generous," he said.

"I'm considering firing Claudia," she said.

"Great idea," he agreed.

Her head snapped up. "You agree?"

"Absolutely, get rid of her. She's a great second assistant, but you need to get her out of the way so you can rehire Holly, right?" Gideon turned back to his desk and picked up another stack of photographs.

"Of all the ridiculous notions, really, Gideon," Victoria sighed.

"Of course, that would be quite ridiculous," he agreed. He placed his glasses back on and selected a photograph, holding it up to get a better angle of light. "Because, if you think about it, Holly might not want, or even be able to do, the job. After all, if you think about it, a series of unfortunate events led her to work at *Arrival* in the first place. Would she have chosen to work here? No. Is she interested in fashion? No. Was she good at her job? Absolutely, yes. Would she be capable of doing her job now? Questionable."

He lowered the photo and picked up another.

"If you think about it, this is a fresh start for her. A chance that a lot of people would kill for. Brain injury aside, she has a chance to examine what she really wants from life and to start over. Isn't that priceless? Especially if you were doing something you didn't love." He lowered the photo and peered at Victoria. "Don't you agree?"

She sighed. "Yes," she whispered.

Gideon smiled sadly. "I know you want to turn back

time and put everything back the way it was. But you can't. Holly won't work here again, you need to leave her to her own devices to find a new path. Whatever that may be."

"I can offer her a job, safe employment, a salary."

"Handcuffing her to her old life," Gideon pointed out.

"I…" She trailed off.

"You?"

"I… just want to help," she admitted.

"Sometimes, help comes in the form of space and time." He regarded her silently for a moment, wondering if now was the time to ask. "Can I ask you a question?"

Victoria shrugged her shoulder slightly. He took it as agreement.

"Let's say, god forbid, Louise gets hit by a taxi. Total amnesia. Would Louise be convalescing at Chez Hastings?"

"No, of course not." Victoria rolled her eyes. "Louise has family. And presumably this is a New York taxi, so she wouldn't have to be stranded in Paris for a year!"

"So, is Holly staying with you because of the guilty you feel?" he pressed.

Victoria took in a slow, deep breath while she considered the question.

"I suppose so, yes," she confessed. "I do feel that there was more I could have done. No, *should* have done. Once Holly walked away… I should have done something."

"You couldn't have known…"

"She was in a foreign country because of me. I was ultimately responsible for her well-being. I dropped the ball." Victoria stepped down from the stool and paced the room. "What kind of person doesn't even check that her assistant got home safely? Even if she did abandon me in my hour of need?"

Gideon watched Victoria pace. Before Holly had gone missing, he'd had a suspicion about something. Now he was surer than ever.

"I have another question," he said.

She stopped pacing and looked at him.

"Is it *just* guilt?"

Victoria blinked. "What do you mean?"

"This protectiveness you clearly feel for her… is it just because of guilt or do you maybe have deeper feelings for Holly in particular? Deeper than you might for someone else in that situation?"

Victoria looked at her watch and rolled her eyes at the passage of time. "Will you come to the house tomorrow evening for dinner?" She casually glossed over his question. "I'd like to slowly reintroduce Holly to her *Arrival* colleagues to see if any memories return."

"I'd love to," Gideon replied. Clearly the topic was closed for discussion. Which meant only one thing, he'd touched a nerve.

"Good, I'll contact you later regarding times." The editor turned on her heel and marched from the office.

CHAPTER TWENTY-THREE

Victoria walked up the steps to her house. A text from Holly had asked what time she expected to be home. Curious to know how Holly had got on that day, she'd given a time far earlier than she ordinarily would have.

She opened the front door and was greeted by delicious smells. She placed her coat in the closet, greedily inhaling the aromas wafting from the kitchen. She often used the services of a chef when the children were home and she was working late, but Carina was having a well-deserved vacation. Which meant that either Holly was cooking, or a very cheeky thief was helping themselves to her pantry.

Victoria crossed the entrance hall and leaned on the doorway of the kitchen, a smile on her face as she took in the scene.

Holly had annihilated the kitchen. Shopping bags, packaging, ingredients, and an abundance of either flour or sugar covered the work surface.

"A year in Paris and this is the legacy," Victoria joked.

Holly spun around in surprise.

"You're home!" She smiled. "It looks worse than it is, and I swear I'll clean it up when I'm done."

"Done doing what?" Victoria questioned.

"Cooking you a meal." Holly beamed. "Three courses, you better be hungry."

Victoria took a step into the room and started to inspect what was on the work surface.

"No looking," Holly chastised. "Go and sit over there, or go and get changed into an eating outfit…"

Victoria rolled her eyes good-humouredly. She walked over to the table and sat down.

"I'll sit here and watch you further destroy my kitchen, if I'm allowed?"

Holly ignored the comment and removed a large saucepan from the hob. "I had the best day."

"Wonderful, everything went well?" Victoria felt a weight lift off her shoulders at the news.

"Yes. My new doctors are great. We've figured out a schedule for physiotherapy, and we are going to try some new memory recovery techniques. Michael, your lawyer, was great. He found that I had three bank accounts, two were practically empty but the third actually had some money in it. So, I have money." She curtsied.

"Congratulations." Victoria couldn't help but smile at the enthusiasm radiating from Holly.

"Yeah, it seems I was good with money because I had some savings. So, I thought I'd cook you a nice dinner to celebrate and say thank you."

"I keep telling you, you don't need to thank me."

"Okay, make yourself useful and set the table then," Holly joked.

Victoria chuckled. She stood up and picked out some cutlery.

"Oh, and I have stuff in storage. Well, I hope I do. I have a storage locker, so that's cool."

"Very cool," Victoria said with a smirk.

"Oh, and I have very big news. Very exciting stuff," Holly said.

Victoria placed a wine glass on the table. "Oh?"

"Yes, I have a date!"

"I'm fine," Victoria muttered through gritted teeth.

"Let me see," Holly insisted. She took Victoria's clenched hand and inspected the bloody wound. She pulled Victoria over to the sink and put the cold tap on.

"It doesn't look too deep," Holly said as she put Victoria's hand under the stream of water. "Where's the first aid kit?"

"It's fine," Victoria repeated.

Holly glared at her.

"The cupboard in the hallway bathroom, second door on the left."

Holly vanished in search of the first aid kit, and Victoria looked at her damaged palm in disgust.

"That wine glass just shattered," Holly said as she returned.

"Yes, it was old. The dishwasher must have cracked it," Victoria lied. "Anyway, you were saying you had news?"

Holly pulled Victoria's hand out from under the tap.

She gently dabbed a towel around the wound and started to wrap a bandage around her hand.

"Oh, yes, I have a date. Tomorrow evening," Holly explained with a wide grin.

"Wow," Victoria said with forced enthusiasm to try to match Holly's glee. "That's soon, isn't it?"

Holly shrugged. "I suppose so. But you only live once, so why not? You know what I mean?" She tightened the bandage.

"Not really," Victoria muttered.

"Sorry, what?" Holly asked.

"Thank you," Victoria said louder. "For the bandage. Who… is your date?" She gave her best faux smile.

"Someone I met in Michael's office, he's one of the junior partners, David. He was really nice, and we hit it off." Holly cleaned her hands. "That is okay, isn't it? You didn't have plans, did you?"

Victoria shook her head. "No. No plans. I… I thought you dated women?"

Holly considered the question and then shrugged her shoulders. "I never thought about it. I suppose I'm bisexual." She turned around and continued with the meal preparation.

"Excuse me, I have to change into my eating outfit," Victoria deadpanned.

She walked out of the kitchen, eager to get some space. She couldn't believe that Holly was already dating. She tried to recall a David at Michael's office, but all the young men just blurred into one poorly-suited stereotype. She wondered if her power of attorney gave her authority to cancel the date. Surely it was too soon?

She'd barely approached the stairs when the doorbell rang. Suddenly she remembered the other reason she was home early that evening.

She turned and walked towards the front door, at the same time Holly appeared from the kitchen.

"I'm sorry, I completely forgot about this," Victoria confessed.

She opened the door, and a large Newfoundland came bounding into the house. She thanked the dog sitter and closed the front door again. When she turned around the dog was already barking happily at Holly.

"Down, girl!" Holly instructed with a smile. "That's enough, Izzy, quiet now."

Izzy sat down obediently, her large tail wagging loudly on the floor.

Victoria stared at Holly in stunned silence.

Holly's eyes widened as she realised what she had said. She stared in shock at the dog and whispered, "Izzy…"

Izzy panted with excitement, looking from one silent woman to the other.

Victoria finally broke the silence. "Y-you… You. Remember. The. *Dog?*" she asked in disbelief.

"I don't choose what I remember!" Holly defended.

Victoria stared at her for a few more moments before she shook her head. She turned and walked up the stairs.

CHAPTER TWENTY-FOUR

Holly leaned over the bannister rail and looked up the stairway towards the third floor of the townhouse. It had been a couple of hours since Victoria had left, and there was no sign that she intended to return.

Holly had never been upstairs. It seemed like a private space for the family. Somewhere she might not be welcome, especially if the look on Victoria's face was anything to go by.

She'd tried calling up the stairs and even sent text messages, but she was met with stony silence.

Since Victoria had stormed off, Holly had finished preparing the meal and placed it in containers in the fridge. She'd then cleaned the kitchen and returned everything to the exact way she had found it.

Now she wondered what course of action to take. Going up the stairs seemed like a very bad idea. She'd just have to wait for Victoria to come down. Surely, she must be hungry? Or maybe she had a kitchen up there on one of the hundred floors? Or maybe her children had chocolate stashed away in their rooms? Holly grinned at the thought of Victoria raiding a child's chocolate supply rather than coming downstairs.

Holly couldn't imagine Victoria giving up easily. Deciding that she'd wasted enough time, she turned the lights off and started to head down to her basement guest area.

As she was halfway down the stairs, she heard a key in the front door. She stood still and listened to the noises in the darkness. She wondered if Victoria had somehow managed to evade her and left the house.

She crept up the stairs so she could hear if it was Victoria returning to the house or a murderer who happened to have a key.

She heard the door creak open and then close again with a small click.

Heels clacked across the hardwood floor towards Victoria's study at the back of the house. Holly pressed herself against the bannister and held her breath as the person passed. She crept a little higher up the stairs and peeked through the spindles.

The streetlight filtered through the glass of the front door and cast a light on a young woman, dressed in a long coat. The woman placed something on the telephone table just outside of Victoria's office. She straightened the flowers in the vase on the table and took a step back to evaluate the scene. She stepped forward again and moved a single bloom half a centimetre and then straightened whatever she had placed on the table top.

She nodded to herself and quickly turned around,

glancing up the stairwell with much the same terror that Holly felt.

A few moments later, she was gone.

Holly climbed the stairs and walked over to the table. A large ring-bound book with ARRIVAL written in large letters across the front sat on the table.

She immediately recognised it as the famous Book, a mock-up of the next issue of *Arrival*. Apparently one of her jobs had been to wait late in the office for the final copy of the Book and then deliver it to Victoria at home. Victoria would then work on it overnight and return it the next morning with changes.

Holly picked up the Book, looked towards the stairs, and smiled a large, evil smile.

Holly felt herself being pulled back into consciousness. Despite her sleep-riddled mind, she clutched her precious cargo tighter to her chest.

She opened her eyes and saw Victoria standing over her, trying to pull the Book out from under her folded arms. Distractedly she wondered how much time had gone by since she sat in the comfortable armchair in Victoria's office, holding the Book. Clearly a while if she had managed to fall into a deep sleep.

"Give me the Book," Victoria mumbled. "You're impossible."

"Yep, I don't remember much, but I do remember that much about me," Holly agreed.

Victoria was leaning over her, using her height over the

seated Holly as an advantage as she pulled on the Book. Holly held the Book in a full-body bear hug to prevent it from being taken.

"I need to work," Victoria grunted in frustration.

"We need to talk," Holly countered.

"There's nothing to say." Victoria released her grip on the Book and stood with her hands on her hips, glaring down at Holly.

"Yes, there is," Holly argued. "I've upset you, and I want to apologise."

"The best apology would be to give me the Book." Victoria dived forward to grab it.

"I'm sorry that I remembered Izzy and not you," Holly said. She gripped the Book with all her might. "It just came out. I don't remember anything specific. Just in the heat of the moment, I knew her name."

Victoria let go of the Book. She took a step back and sighed as she pinched the bridge of her nose.

"Yes, I know," she whispered.

Holly let out a small sigh of relief.

Finally, the editor was caving in. Willing to talk. Kind of.

"Although my memories aren't flooding back, I am getting… sensations, feelings about things," Holly explained. "I can't explain, but I have this very strong feeling about you. I know you. I know you were important in my life."

Victoria gave a derisive laugh but looked somewhat pleased to hear the admission.

"Remembering Izzy's name means those memories must be in there somewhere, right? A part of the memory centre must still be functioning." Holly smiled. "I'll remember you, I promise."

"No, no…" Victoria shook her head sadly. "You shouldn't make such promises. You may not be able to do so. Yes, remembering Izzy's name is positive news, but you have to take it one step at a time."

"I'm sorry if I hurt you," Holly said softly.

"It's been a trying day," Victoria confessed.

Holly assumed that was as much of an apology as she'd ever get from the woman. Victoria looked tired and emotionally worn out.

"Would you like something to eat?" Holly asked, hoping to snag a few more minutes with her.

Victoria shook her head. She was clearly not ready to commit to full forgiveness just yet.

"No, thank you. I think I will have a look at the Book and then have an early night."

Holly smiled sadly. She held the Book up, and Victoria accepted it with a grateful nod. She turned around and headed for the stairs.

"Good night, Victoria," Holly whispered after her.

CHAPTER TWENTY-FIVE

Gideon glanced up to see Victoria open the glass door to his office. She glided into the room and took her customary place on the stool. He could tell something was wrong, by the solemn look on her face.

"Good morning," Gideon greeted. He continued to focus on his work, hand-drawing the feature page layout with a mechanical pencil.

"I just came in to say that dinner is… delayed," Victoria said in a soft tone.

There was clearly more on her mind. Gideon knew he wouldn't have to wait long before she spilled whatever it was. Until that time, he intended to continue working to meet the ridiculous deadline she'd imposed upon him.

Victoria was known for handing out stacks of work to be completed in impossibly short amounts of time. That was fine if you were one of the ninety-nine percent of people Victoria didn't give a second glance to. But as the closest thing she had to a friend, Gideon had to also balance

Victoria's occasional desire to confess what was on her mind.

Not that he made it easy. One of the reasons Victoria opened up to him was because he rarely asked any direct questions. He held back and waited for her to tell him whatever was on her mind.

"Oh, well, let me know when it's back on," he said without looking up.

Victoria sat in silence for a few moments before speaking again.

"Holly has made other plans."

"Ah," Gideon said. "Well, another night then."

"She has a date, Gideon. A date!"

He sighed and put the pencil in the pot on his desk.

"I see." He removed his glasses and started to clean the lenses.

"What? What do you see?" Victoria glared at him, seeming to be spoiling for a fight.

"That Holly has a date," he replied with a placating smile.

"Why on earth are you smiling, Gideon? Dinner is cancelled." Victoria used the same tone Gideon imagined she'd use to announce the end of days.

"Well, ours is. It seems someone will still be having dinner," he pointed out.

"She doesn't even know him, of course. And she remembers the damn dog."

He frowned. "He has a dog?"

"No, Gideon." She sighed with exasperation. "Try to keep up. She remembers Izzy."

"So, she remembers *your* dog? That's wonderful news."

Gideon smiled, but the expression soon slipped from his face when he saw Victoria's was still thundery. "Or, apparently not?"

"I'm afraid I don't see what's so wonderful about it." She shook her head in dismay.

"Well, the fact that she has managed to recover any memories at all is a good thing. And the fact that she remembered your dog, which is a direct connection to you." He held his glasses up to the light to check they were spotlessly clean.

"Why would that matter?" Victoria sniffed.

"I don't know, I just thought I'd mention it." He couldn't believe how deep-down Victoria had buried her emotions.

"She doesn't even know him," she repeated.

"We're back to the date again, yes?"

Victoria replied with another glare, and he chuckled.

"I fail to see what is so amusing," Victoria said icily.

"Nothing," Gideon continued to smile. "Let me know when our dinner is rearranged." He picked up his pencil and returned to his sketch.

"You clearly have something to say. Out with it," she ordered.

He looked up at her. "For some reason, and I'll allow you to come to your own conclusion on this, you are jealous."

Victoria looked shocked before she blurted out, "Preposterous!"

"If you say so." He turned away and focused on his work.

"Never have I ever heard anything so ridiculous,"

Victoria grumbled. She slid off the stool and stalked over to his desk. She angrily pointed at the design. "That needs to change. I told you before, no more wind machines. Blowing the models around like that. They'll snap like twigs. Really, Gideon."

He felt the draft of the door as she left and heard her heels disappearing down the corridor. He let out a long sigh.

Victoria prowled the corridors of *Arrival*. She delivered piercing glares to anyone who dared to look up at her. She couldn't get the thought of Holly's date out of her mind. She knew Gideon was right, but she'd be damned if she'd admit it to anyone, even to herself.

She turned on her heel and stalked back towards her own office. As she walked along the carpeted hallway, she heard Louise and Claudia in conversation. She could tell from their hushed tones that it was something juicy. Probably about her. She slowed her pace and waited around the corner to listen.

"It's disgusting," Louise whispered.

"It isn't right," Claudia agreed.

Victoria crept a little closer. If her two assistants were talking about her, then she wanted to catch them in the act.

"He's fifty for God's sake," Louise said, despair clear in her voice.

"And she's how old?" Claudia asked.

"Thirty," Louise spat. "It's disgusting. Twenty years between them. They can't have anything in common. No, it's just an old person wanting to have a young person as a trophy."

"It makes me feel queasy," Claudia said.

"It makes you feel queasy?" Louise snorted a bitter laugh. "Imagine how I feel. I have to sit across from them at a restaurant and watch them… together."

Victoria swallowed. She took a step backwards and pressed up against the wall, her legs shaking slightly.

"Why do old people do it?" Claudia asked.

"Don't ask me," Louise replied. "Surely they must know that they are laughingstocks? Drooling over someone half their age."

Victoria felt her cheeks flush. She had heard enough. She pushed herself away from the wall and walked away.

Gideon approached Victoria's office with every intention of begging on bended knee because, dammit, he really needed that wind machine. As he approached the outer office, he could see she wasn't there.

He looked at Louise with a raised eyebrow and gestured towards Victoria's office.

"Where?" he questioned.

"No idea. We're enjoying the peace," Louise said. Her phone chirped and she sighed. "Well, almost peace. Parents!"

"What's wrong?" Gideon asked.

Louise ignored him and started to type out a response on her phone. He turned to Claudia and raised an inquisitive eyebrow.

"Her dad is dating a new woman," Claudia replied, typing without looking up. "She is much younger than him, and Louise's mom has flipped."

"They've been divorced for six years," Louise explained. "But Mom is being awful. I just don't want to know. I mean, he's dating someone who is only three years older than me. I don't want to hear about it."

"It is gross, though," Claudia said. "He's fifty and she's thirty."

The young girls shuddered.

"Well, sometimes an age gap works. Depends on the personality types," Gideon said.

Claudia looked at him curiously.

"It's true," he defended his statement. "Not that I'm dating anyone younger than me. Dating is a distant memory, anyway."

"You think it's okay for someone to date someone half their age?" Claudia questioned.

"I think it's up to the individuals. Who are we to judge?" he replied. "Sometimes people just click, and age has nothing to do with it. Let me ask you a question, would you rather be in a relationship with someone twice your age that you absolutely adored, who was perfect for you in every way, or someone your own age who didn't share any of your interests and treated you badly?"

"Well, of course I'd want the person I loved," Claudia replied.

"Of course you would. That's all any of us want. Age is a number. No two twenty-year-olds are the same. No two fifty-year-olds are the same. It's one of those ridiculous social constructs that tell us what we should and shouldn't do. I would have expected young women like you two to know better."

The tips of Claudia's ears turned red. She nodded her head, clearly ashamed by her judgemental attitude.

Serves you right, Gideon thought.

"Anyway, you have no idea where Victoria is?"

"Nope," Louise said. "She's been gone a while."

"She has no meetings and her coat and bag are still here, so she must be in the building somewhere," Claudia offered. She took a sip of the kombucha on her desk and slipped her headphones on.

Gideon had spent thirty minutes checking every potential location within the *Arrival* offices. Except one. And with that one location the only place he hadn't checked, he knew she must be there.

He pushed on the door of the executive ladies' washroom so hard that it cracked loudly against the wall. Victoria, who had been standing looking at her reflection in the mirrors above the sinks, jumped. She spun around, her hand over her heart, and glared at Gideon.

"Found you," Gideon drawled. "Now, I'll go hide and you count to ten."

She shook her head and turned back towards the sink. She leaned heavily on the unit and stared at the mirror again.

"I'm too old for such foolishness, Gideon," she muttered. "Entirely too old."

"Oh, come on, you're not old." He strolled over to the

other side of the room, folded his arms, and leaned against the wall. He met her eyes in the mirror.

"I am, Gideon." She turned around and looked at him with an expression of dead seriousness. "I'm having a midlife crisis."

"I thought you were sixty hundred and sixty-six years old?" he joked.

She cracked a smile. "As you well know, that Wikipedia edit was a prank performed by one of the many second assistants whom I've fired."

"Ah."

"However old I am," she continued with a sigh, "it's clearly old. I'm having a midlife crisis. Aren't you supposed to be supportive during this time of mental anguish?"

"You're not having a midlife crisis," he told her. "What makes you think you are?"

"Everything," she said unhelpfully.

He raised an eyebrow and patiently waited for her to continue.

"I don't know," she admitted. "I'm confused. Emotional. My mind is playing tricks on me. I need you to take over *Arrival* for a while. Think of it as a practice run for our succession plans."

"No." Gideon shook his head.

"What do you mean, no?" she demanded. "I'm having a midlife crisis, support me!"

"For the last time, you're not having a midlife crisis," he assured her. "You're suddenly becoming aware that you care for Holly and you don't like it. In fact, I'm guessing that you more than care for her."

"Gideon," she warned.

"And, as a result, you're thinking about your age. And its relation to *her* age."

"Gideon," she warned again.

"Is it so awful?" he asked. "Caring for her?"

"It is when we all know that one day her memories will return, and she'll see me for who I am. I can accept that she has no feelings for me. Life happens, sometimes people don't feel the same way. But I don't want to see fear and hatred in her eyes. That will break me."

Ah, so that's it, Gideon realised.

"You think she's going to remember working for you?" he asked.

"Of course she will. It's just a matter of time. She's remembered Izzy. Slowly but surely the rest will come. Right now, it's all locked away in that pretty little head."

Gideon didn't have an answer for that. Victoria may be right. He wasn't about to try to convince her otherwise.

"It's Friday, go home and rest for the weekend. See how you feel on Monday. If you truly are having a midlife crisis then I will, of course, take over," he said.

He pushed away from the wall to walk towards his employer and friend.

"Victoria… don't push her away. Whatever it is you're feeling. Don't lose her again."

"I… I won't." She lowered her head.

"Good, call me if you need me."

He made his move to leave. As he passed her, he gently brushed his hand against hers.

He left her alone, hoping that she wouldn't let fear lead her. Victoria liked to give the impression that she was a strong and fearless woman, but Gideon knew that she was actually a sensitive person.

He'd long since suspected that Victoria felt something for Holly, but he was surprised at Victoria's casual admission of it. Even though she had told him of her feelings, he knew it would be a wintery day in Hell before she told anyone else. Specifically, Holly herself.

He couldn't blame her for being afraid of what Holly's potential memories could do to their new friendship. Their working relationship had been fraught, to say the least.

Gideon had no idea what would happen next. Holly had cared about Victoria to some degree, she'd admitted as much to him before she left. But what form that care took, and whether or not it still existed, was another matter entirely.

He smirked ruefully as he took the elevator back to his office. He didn't envy the situation either woman was in.

CHAPTER TWENTY-SIX

HOLLY OPENED the front door to the townhouse as quietly as she could. She turned and waved goodbye to David. He'd insisted on walking her home but steadfastly refused to even climb the stairs in case he met Victoria. Holly had spent much of the dinner reassuring him that she wasn't being held against her will in the Hastings house.

At first, she had thought he was being silly and overreacting, but when she remembered the news articles she had found online, and her own overreaction, she could see where he was coming from. Since she'd lived with Victoria, she had quickly discovered that the woman was very different than the myth.

David waved back and offered her a smile. He dug his hands into his pockets and turned to walk away.

Holly stepped inside and closed the door. She leaned against the doorframe to remove her high heels. Getting used to wearing the demon footwear was a long process, and she'd need to practise. She'd only worn the shoes for a couple of short walks – and tonight she had spent most of her time either in a taxi or at the restaurant – and she was already limping.

She noticed a dim light coming from Victoria's study door. She crossed the hallway, noting the untouched Arrival Book on the telephone table. It seemed curious that Victoria was in her office but not working. She peeked around the corner.

Victoria was sitting in the armchair, her legs curled beneath her, wrapped in a sinfully soft-looking blanket. She was reading a book. The light above her seat bathed the room in a cosy glow. The whole scene looked heavenly comfortable.

"Did you have a nice evening?" Victoria asked without looking up.

Holly smiled. She wasn't as stealthy as she thought. She walked into the room and sat on the sofa beside the armchair.

"Yes, it was very nice. He's a nice guy."

"Good." Victoria continued to read her book.

Holly angled her head but couldn't quite see the book cover. "What are you reading?"

Victoria lifted the book up slightly.

"Dickens!"

Victoria nodded. "Yes, it occurred to me that I haven't read this since I was a little girl, many, many years ago. *Bleak House* was always my favourite Dickens."

It was obvious that, while Victoria's mood had improved, something was still off. Holly doubted Victoria was the kind of person who would want to open up and talk about it.

"Can I get you a drink? Some tea?" Holly offered.

Victoria shook her head. "No, thank you."

"Have you eaten?" Holly knew she wasn't doing a good job at hiding the concern in her voice.

Victoria placed her book in her lap and smiled. "Actually, I have. I ate some of the delicious meal you prepared yesterday. Clearly you are an accomplished chef."

Holly felt her cheeks blush. "No, I'm just good at following instructions."

"Well, it was delicious. Thank you." Victoria cleared her throat. "Gideon, a dear friend and work colleague, would love to come over and meet you sometime soon. If that is acceptable?"

Holly was excited about the prospect of meeting someone from her past. "Absolutely, I'm free whenever he is!"

"No more dates with Darren?" Victoria enquired, smoothing the blanket that covered her feet.

"David," Holly corrected with a smile. "No, no more dates with David."

Victoria frowned. "I thought you said you had a nice evening?"

"Oh, I did," Holly replied. "As I said, he is a really nice guy. I just didn't feel anything for him, like that, I mean."

"Oh, I see."

"So, who is Gideon?" Holly pressed.

"Gideon is my director of photography. But really, he is my right-hand man, invaluable. And a wonderful friend of many years. You worked with him extensively, and I'm led to believe that you were also rather close. Certainly closer than most of your other work colleagues. Gideon took you under his wing when you started at *Arrival*, showed you the ropes, etcetera."

Holly bit her lip with excitement. She was thrilled with the chance to meet someone who knew her, someone who could give her more insight into herself.

"Great, whenever Gideon wants to meet up, that would be great. Except tomorrow morning."

"What's happening tomorrow morning?" Victoria asked.

"I get the key to the storage unit." Holly blew out a nervous breath. She didn't know if the unit would be full of trash or treasure. It would be a long and sleepless night before she found out.

"I see. Would you like some company?"

Holly felt her shoulders slump with relief. She'd wanted to ask for Victoria's moral support, but she was nervous to do so in light of recent events.

"Yes, I really would love you to be there," she admitted.

Victoria smiled, the first real smile Holly had seen from her in a while.

"What time would you like to be there?" Victoria asked.

"The office opens at nine, and I kind of wanted to be there first thing. It's by Central Park, West Eighty-Fourth."

Victoria's eyes flicked towards the ceiling as she calculated the information. "We'll leave at quarter to nine. That gives us plenty of time. And I'll take the Range."

"R-range? As in Range Rover?"

"Yes, in case you want to bring anything back," Victoria clarified.

Holly had never thought of Victoria as a driver, much

less a New York driver. As far as she knew, the woman was always chauffeured.

"Thank you, I really appreciate that," Holly said in earnest. She couldn't believe how lucky she was. Victoria had found her, rescued her, and continued to help and support her. Yes, she was a little frosty at times, but Holly could see that it was mainly an act.

"I was just about to head to bed," Victoria said. She started to stand up.

"Oh, you looked so comfortable. I was going to grab a book of my own and join you."

Victoria folded the blanket and placed it on the back of the armchair. "Feel free to use the room, I've had a long day and an early night is on the cards."

Holly didn't believe her for one moment, but she allowed the older woman her escape. "Okay, good night."

Victoria picked up her book and nodded her own good night.

Holly stretched her arms up and wondered what to do. She knew she wouldn't be able to sleep. She had genuinely been considering reading, but mainly to be with Victoria. After spending so much time with her, she now found she missed her company.

She stood up and walked over to the bookshelves. There was no order to the books that Holly could discern. They were from various authors and in various genres. The only common theme was that they were all specially bound, artistic special editions.

Another bookcase was filled with back issues of *Arrival* Magazine. She picked one up at random, pulling the one beside it out to act as a marker. She opened the edition and saw Victoria's face staring back at her beside the Editor's Letter for that month. She read through the letter and chuckled at the light tone and jokes. She slowly walked over to the armchair, her nose still in the magazine.

Victoria knew she was asleep. She knew she was dreaming. And yet she was powerless to stop the narrative from playing out. In her dream, she was asleep in bed, much the same as in real life. She could feel that strange dreamlike aura, that fuzzy confusion that prevents one from quite grasping onto reality.

In the dream, the creaking of the bedroom door woke her. She noticed the lamp on the bedside table was on, which was unusual. She never left it on while she slept. The light enabled her to see Holly in the doorway.

Her mouth instantly ran dry.

Holly entered the bedroom, one hand leaning casually on the doorframe. She was dressed in Victoria's favourite couture from the Aubade 2015 collection. Holly's long hair curled around her pale shoulders, and Victoria distantly wondered when the girl had grown her hair again.

"Shh," Holly hushed before Victoria had the chance to form a cohesive sentence.

Victoria sat up in bed, pulling the sheets with her to keep herself covered. At least one of them should be worried about decency.

"What's all this nonsense about a midlife crisis?" Holly asked as she sauntered into the bedroom.

Victoria stared in shock as Holly approached the end of

the bed, staring at Victoria with what could only be described as ravenous hunger.

"That feeling in your stomach, the one you attribute to guilt," Holly whispered. "You know that's not guilt, don't you?"

Victoria swallowed hard and reminded herself that this was a dream.

Holly climbed up the bed too quickly for her to protest. In a matter of seconds, she had straddled Victoria. She leant her elbows on either side of Victoria, close enough for Victoria to feel the heat pulsing from her lingerie-clad body through the sheet.

"You know that's desire, don't you? You desire me, Victoria. Don't you?"

Victoria woke up with a jolt. She sat upright in her empty bed, heavy breaths falling from her open mouth. Her eyes raced around the darkness to assure herself that she was alone.

"Oh, shit," she murmured.

CHAPTER TWENTY-SEVEN

VICTORIA WOKE EARLY the next morning to catch up on some work with the Book. The previous evening she had been too preoccupied by Holly's absence to get anything done. She'd constantly wondered how her date was going and debated how insane she'd seem if she texted Holly to ask if she was okay. Dickens had eventually come to her salvation and kept her entertained, well, distracted, until Holly had returned.

But now it was time to work.

Especially after the unwelcome dream last night. She was a firm believer in using work to suppress one's feelings. For years, Victoria had reaped the benefits of burying herself in work as an avoidance tactic.

Of course, she enjoyed her work and was incredibly proud of what she had achieved during her time at *Arrival*. But she had noticed parallels between her life and her work output. She could catalogue most of her life events through *Arrival* issues, layouts, trends, models, revenue, and circulation numbers.

Most people would remember the death of a parent by the year. Victoria remembered her father's death as the sixteen-page spread on sixties revival haircuts, shoes, and hemlines. The birth of her son Hugo was marked by the launch of the new website. Her daughter Alexia by the new font for the iconic headline. The death of her marriage was marked by the worst advertising revenue month in history. Poetic, in a way.

She tried to throw herself into her work now, but she found it difficult. Her mind was unfocused. It was taking longer than ever to go through the Book. Her wastepaper bin was overflowing with screwed-up Post-It notes that marked where she changed her mind.

Eventually she threw her pen down and gave up. She looked at her watch. It was a mere forty-five minutes before they were due to leave for the storage locker. She sighed and removed her glasses. She closed her eyes and leaned back in her chair, trying to gather her thoughts.

She wondered what the storage locker would hold. According to Gideon, Holly had just broken up with her girlfriend before leaving for Paris. There was a chance that a wealth of memory-evoking materials was hoarded away in the locker.

She found herself wondering about Holly's memory of Izzy. Why did she remember the dog? It wasn't like they had spent a lot of time together. There was the time Victoria had sent her to the vet after Izzy had eaten an entire bowl of fruit and contracted chronic diarrhoea. She didn't want to see her pet in pain, but she also didn't want to accompany her as she knew it would be a messy job. Sending Holly, who she had been punishing at the time, seemed like a good compromise all around.

She supposed that was something that wouldn't easily be forgotten. Then again, she'd also taken Izzy to be groomed on several occasions and had claimed to have enjoyed it.

Was Izzy a good memory or a bad one? Did memory retrieval work like that? She had no idea.

She smiled smugly to herself. In the whole of New York, Holly had only recalled Izzy to date. There was a small sense of satisfaction. Holly had remembered something close to Victoria, and that was something to be happy about.

"Victoria?"

She opened her eyes and saw Holly standing in the doorway.

"I'm not disturbing you, am I?"

"Not at all," Victoria replied. She sat forward and pulled the Book towards her to at least pretend she had gotten some work done.

"How did you sleep?" Holly asked.

Victoria hoped her blush wasn't visible. "Well, yourself?"

"I was awake most of the night," Holly admitted.

"Oh? Any particular reason?"

"I think I'm nervous about what I'll find today."

You and me both, Victoria thought. "I'm sure it will be fine. How about some breakfast to settle your stomach?"

Holly tucked a lock of hair behind her ear. "That would be nice. Join me?"

Victoria meant to say no, but somehow found she was already on her feet.

The journey to the storage unit was made in silence. Holly was nervous and didn't know what to say. She could also detect a strange mood in Victoria. She was desperate to not have another disagreement, they had started to get back to normal and she didn't want to make things worse.

She'd managed to convince Victoria to eat breakfast with her, but that, too, had been a silent affair. She just didn't know where she stood with the elusive woman, and she longed for the Victoria she first met in Paris to return.

Luckily, it didn't take long before they were pulling into the parking lot of the large storage facility.

"Wow, I hope they don't expect me to remember the unit number," Holly mumbled as she looked out of the window.

They walked into the lobby, which was a cramped area selling boxes, tape, and an assortment of moving equipment. Behind the desk was a tall man with a scruffy beard. He wore a bright red T-shirt and baseball cap, both emblazoned with the company logo.

"Hey, long time, no see," he said when he saw Holly. "You cut your hair. Looks awesome."

"Er, thanks," Holly said hesitantly as she approached the desk.

"We thought you'd vanished. Normally we would have sold it off, but the boss said he had a feeling you'd be back. Carter, isn't it?"

Holly nodded. "Yes, Holly Carter."

The man smiled warmly and started to type on a computer.

"Carter, Carter… yep. Here we are. All right." He picked up a calculator. "That's twelve months, minus your initial payment and deposit, plus the tax, plus the security, and then the lost key." He looked up. "I presume you don't have your key?"

Holly shook her head apologetically.

"Plus the lost key, a new key, a month up front." He continued to tap on the calculator. "Right, that will be two thousand, six hundred and forty-three dollars. Oh, and eighty cents." He turned the calculator around so Holly could see the eye-watering amount.

"W-what?"

He leaned forward to look at the calculator. "Two thousand, six hundred—"

"Yes, I heard. Wow. Um. I… I don't have that money. Well, I do but it would wipe out my savings," Holly admitted. "I was in an accident, amnesia. I had no idea I had this storage locker and I think my entire life is in it… I really need to see it."

He nodded in sad understanding. "Yeah, but it's been twelve months since the last payment. You said you'd be back in two weeks, so we put you on a rolling plan in a long-term unit when you didn't show. There's an admin charge and a moving charge for that. Our long-term units have twenty-four-hour security to protect your belongings. And you lost your key, so there's a fee for that, and a fee for a new one."

"Look, I literally just got out of the hospital—"

"I'm sorry, I can't give you access until the account has been paid up."

"Can I… can I set up a payment plan or something?" Holly tried.

An American Express black card was slapped down onto the desk.

"Pay the account. Get me the key. Chop chop," Victoria said.

"Is she with you?" he asked, looking from Holly to Victoria.

Holly ignored him and looked at Victoria. "You don't have to do this. I can figure out another way—"

Victoria ignored Holly. "Yes, I am with her." She peered at his name badge. "Charge my card and get me the key, Terry."

Terry grabbed the card and started to input data into his computer.

"Victoria, please, I already owe you so much…" Holly said.

Victoria looked at Holly, her expression softened. "You don't owe me anything."

Holly licked her dry lips. "I do, I owe you… everything."

"That's not how I see it," Victoria said.

"Unit seventy-two." Terry placed a key on the desk with a large wooden block attached to it.

Victoria picked up the key and eyed the wooden block with distaste.

"Out of the doors, go left, second on your right, and then fifth on the left. Everything is signposted." Terry held out Victoria's card.

They worked their way through the maze of corridors in silence. Holly was mentally calculating how much money she must owe Victoria by now and wondered what organs were worth on the black market.

They stopped outside unit seventy-two. Victoria handed Holly the key and looked down to the industrial-strength padlock. Holly took a deep breath and bent down. She unlocked the padlock, released it from the catch, and pushed the door up. The noise echoed loudly down the empty corridors.

She stood up and peered into the dark room. She saw a lit-up button on the wall and pushed it. A bright fluorescent tube sprung to life, flickering a few times before finally illuminating the room.

"It appears," Victoria murmured as she looked around, "that you are a hoarder."

Holly nodded her agreement.

Inside the room were countless boxes, black sacks, and a scattering of furniture.

"There was a part of me that worried there would be nothing in here," Holly confessed.

"Well, you can safely put that fear to bed."

Holly took in the sight. The boxes looked hastily packed. Some were not taped shut, and some had things sticking out of the tops of them. The sacks and carrier bags looked like someone had packed in a hurry and run out of boxes. Nothing was labelled. She looked around in shock, realising the enormity of the task.

"Well, what now?" Victoria asked.

"I don't know. I can't take all of this back to your house. It would take twenty trips, and it would fill your house!"

"Then I suggest we start looking through everything and decide what you would like to take back with you today and what can stay for another time."

"Yeah… yeah… okay." Holly walked a little deeper into the unit, her mind racing. "He remembered me."

"Sorry?" Victoria questioned.

"The guy in the office, he remembered me," Holly said.

"Yes, he did." Victoria stepped into the room and started to look around.

"I wonder why?" Holly asked.

Victoria laughed. "Oh, yes, such a mystery."

"You don't think so?" Holly asked. "Surely he sees hundreds of people?"

Victoria sighed and turned to face her. "Holly, you are a beautiful woman. Of course he remembers you."

Holly felt her cheeks blush. "Oh, I'm not. I've seen your magazine, I'm not beautiful. Those models on the pages of *Arrival*, they're beautiful."

Victoria put on her leather driving gloves and flipped the lid off of a box. "Models exist to be as plain as possible so the clothes get all the attention. Of course, some of them are pretty, if you appreciate a lack of muscle structure and the façade of a face. But, on the whole, no… models are not beautiful. They serve a purpose. They are hangers. Glorified clothes hangers. Well-compensated hangers, but hangers nonetheless. You are a fine example of beauty."

Victoria peered into the box she had opened and then turned to look at Holly. "This box appears to contain old issues of *Arrival*, you certainly don't need them at my house."

Holly stared at Victoria in complete shock. "T-thank

you, Victoria. That means so much to me. Coming from you, of all people."

Victoria looked utterly confused. "Well, of course, I have all the back issues of *Arrival*."

Holly stepped forward and threw her arms around Victoria, encasing her in a hug. Slowly, Victoria brought her own arms up and wrapped them around Holly. Holly smiled, it was clear that Victoria had no idea why she was being hugged. The editor didn't know that her softly spoken speech on what constituted beauty was just what Holly needed to hear.

Something caught Holly's eye sticking out of the top of an opened box. She pulled away from Victoria and gasped with excitement.

"Photo album!" she announced. She picked the album up and held it in the crook of her elbow. She leafed through the pages, memories suddenly hitting her like a shockwave. Not memories as such, but knowledge.

"I remember these people, I remember these photos," she shrieked happily. She turned and threw her arms around Victoria again, this time with the photo album tightly gripped in her right hand.

This time Victoria was quicker to return the embrace and held Holly tightly.

Holly let go and flipped back to the front page of the album. She angled the book to show Victoria. "This is my mom. And that's my maternal nana."

"You remember them?" Victoria breathed.

"Sort of… not everything. Just a sensation of memory. I know I've seen these photos before, I can tell you who these people are, I know… I know some of it. The rest is just out of reach, but I feel like I have a loose thread to pull on."

She flipped through the pages. "I can't believe I couldn't remember these people, my family." She looked up at Victoria with a big smile and tears tracking down her face. "But I remember them now. Bits and pieces anyway."

"It's a start," Victoria told her. "Don't rush it. Clearly your memories are there. Give it time, they will come."

Holly looked down at a photo of herself posing with her parents. Their cheeks were pink, and they all held mugs. She remembered the picture so well, it was taken Christmas. She was fourteen, and it had snowed. They'd made hot chocolate in the evening after spending an hour outside making the best snowman in the world.

"My parents died a while ago," Holly said. "Neither of them had any siblings, and I was an only child, too. So that was that, no family. That's why no one came looking for me, I suspected that was the case, but now I know it."

"Do you need some time alone?" Victoria whispered. She placed a comforting hand on Holly's shoulder.

"No, I'm glad you're here." She sniffed and closed the album. "Let's see what else we can find."

Half an hour later and they had managed to arrange a lot of her possessions into piles. Holly had pushed the furniture into one corner and put all of the sacks and bags of clothing into another. She was taken aback by the amount of clothes she owned. Victoria seemed bewildered that some of those expensive clothes had been consigned to black sacks.

Holly's love of reading had been well and truly confirmed. Many of the boxes contained books. She'd heaved them against a wall, there was no way she would be taking them to Victoria's home as there were enough to fill a modest library.

Luckily, she'd managed to find, and hide, the embarrassing music collection that she just knew she'd possess. Victoria had offered a smirk when she quickly pushed a box of boy band music out from under her probing eye.

The boxes left contained personal items, photographs, a digital camera, a laptop, and an extraordinary number of journals. All of the journals were handwritten by Holly and seemed to document most of her life. If time had been no object, she would have sat down and read them all cover to cover immediately. But she was aware that one of the most important women in publishing was assisting her and probably eager to get home.

"There are more in here," Victoria sounded astonished. She had kicked the lid off of a dusty box with the tip of her heel, and now she pointed down its contents. "You must have thoroughly documented your entire life."

Holly reached into the box and counted the journals. "Twenty-six. That's one for each year of my life."

"I doubt you were chronicling your existence as a baby," Victoria said. She looked Holly up and down. "Although…"

Holly chuckled. "Well, then, I've just had a fascinating life."

"Or you feel the need to write down every single thing that has ever happened to you."

"I prefer my theory." Holly stood up and looked at the boxes that she had decided were essential to take home immediately. "With that one, that's six boxes."

"All right. I'll go and get that imbecile from the office to help us get them to the car," Victoria said.

"I don't think that's his job," Holly commented.

She heard Victoria's snort of laughter as she walked down the corridor and towards the front desk. "I'll be back shortly," she said.

The moment she was gone, Holly picked up a random journal from one of the boxes. The handwriting was messy and there were hand-drawn doodles all over the page. Clearly this was a journal from her youth. She skimmed through a few paragraphs. Apparently young Holly was very excited to be a sheep in the Nativity play.

She put the journal back where she found it and picked up another. The journal was leather-bound, not a paperback like the earlier ones. She flipped through a few pages and finally caught onto the timeline. It was when she had moved to New York but before she worked at *Arrival*. She had a girlfriend named Kate and had aspirations to be a writer. Apparently, she was on her way to being a penniless writer, as she had been turned down for a great many positions already.

She put the journal down and picked up the next one in the sequence. She opened it in the middle. Her handwriting, which had improved in the previous tome, was back to being a mess. There were faint water splotches on the page. Holly read a few lines.

She had started at *Arrival*, and she was miserable. Her life was falling apart and her evil boss, Victoria Hastings, was making her life a living nightmare. She swallowed and closed the book.

There was one last book in the box, presumably the one

she had used before she went away. She picked it up and noticed that there was a bulge from a pen in the middle. She opened the page, gasped in shock, and slammed the book closed again.

She felt her cheeks flare up with heat. She rushed to the corridor to check that no one was around. When she was satisfied that she was alone, she slowly opened the book again. On the page staring up at her was a hand-drawn image of Victoria. Completely naked. She stared at the image and then swallowed hard.

She checked the corridor again. She peeked at the page. She had obviously drawn the picture, but she had no idea if it was from fact or fiction. She couldn't believe what she was seeing. At some point, she had drawn an erotic picture of her boss. Her boss whom she hated just in the last journal. She found herself staring at the image. She licked her dry lips.

She was too shocked to process what she was seeing. And too turned on. It was a vision she hadn't expected, but one she couldn't tear her eyes from.

She heard Victoria's heels clacking down the corridor. She slammed the book closed and buried it under the other journals in the box. She stared at the box for a moment before putting the lid onto top. And then sitting herself on top of the box for good measure.

"He's bringing a cart," Victoria said as she entered the unit. She frowned. "Are you all right? You look flushed."

"I-I'm fine," Holly said quickly.

"Have you done too much? Are your memories retu—"

"I'm fine, just… hungry," Holly lied.

Victoria's eyes narrowed as she tried to ascertain if Holly was unwell or not.

"We'll be home soon, I'm sure we can find you a snack," Victoria offered.

The sound of a trolley rolling in the wrong direction caught their attention. Victoria rolled her eyes and stormed out of the unit.

Holly put her head in her hands.

"Oh, shit," she murmured.

CHAPTER TWENTY-EIGHT

THE JOURNALS WERE LAID out on the ludicrously comfortable guest bed. Holly sat cross-legged in front of them, debating where to start. Her mind had been scrambled ever since she'd seen the suggestive drawing of Victoria.

On the way back, barely a word had been spoken between them. Victoria had asked several times if Holly was okay. Holly had tried to offer assurances that she was fine. Judging from Victoria's displeased expression, she wasn't an accomplished liar.

When they got back, Holly had insisted on carrying the boxes herself. She had almost banned Victoria from even coming near them. She had no idea what other surprises they might contain. Holly was terrified that a flimsy box might break open and spill her secrets at Victoria's feet.

Victoria had skulked off to her office. That left Holly to carry all the boxes to the guestroom and spread out the intriguing journals in front of her. She'd organised them by date order, but nothing more.

She couldn't have possibly wished for more. She had a

complete transcript of all her thoughts, wishes, dreams, desires, sadness, and plans. Written in her own hand.

She'd always suspected that obsessive diary keeping was not just a result of her accident. Now she had proof. She had always compulsively kept diaries.

The first one started when she was eight and received a new pen for Christmas. The last was written about a week before she left for Paris. It seemed she had a habit of writing on scraps of paper and taping them into the main journal, especially when she was travelling. She wondered if she had journaled her time in Paris, that would be a fascinating read.

But she knew she already had enough to get through. She had to decide where to start. Part of her wanted to pick up the most recent journal and work her way backwards. She was desperate to examine the nature of her relationship with her now-former boss.

On the other hand, she didn't want to ignore the rest of her life. Her parents, childhood, schooling, college and beyond. But then the idea of reading solidly for a week just to get to the part where she could uncover her obvious feelings for Victoria didn't appeal to her either.

Her emotions were running high. The sudden flash of recalling her parents and grandparents was fresh in her mind. She couldn't remember everything, just a strong sensation. It was more a feeling of remembering rather than actual recollection. There was still a lot missing, but she felt safer in the knowledge that her memories were in there somewhere.

She let out a deep breath and looked around the guestroom. Victoria was a mystery to her. A delightful one, but a mystery nonetheless. She desperately wanted to know more. She had to know more.

She picked up the journal that fell during the year of her starting at *Arrival*.

The journal taught her about her girlfriend, Kate. The pair had moved to New York with fantastical dreams of making their fortunes. Kate wanted to be a world-renowned chef. Holly wanted to be a world-renowned writer. They rented an apartment in a bad neighbourhood, with an unwavering belief that they would reach their dreams and quickly escape.

It only took a few pages for Kate to be working a low-paid job in a restaurant. It was a rung on the ladder. Sadly, the same wasn't true for Holly. She was turned down for every job she applied for. Money was getting tight.

Kate pressed Holly to take any job to cover their mounting bills and debts. It seemed that, although they had *both* come to New York in search of their dreams, Holly was expected to give up on her ambitions and take whatever job she could get. They fought. A lot.

Holly flipped a few pages on. She couldn't stand to read the despair from her former self. Suddenly, she saw the word "Arrival" and stopped skimming.

She'd been offered a job working for someone named Victoria Hastings. It was obvious she didn't want the job, or even the interview. But it was a last resort and at least somewhere near her chosen field.

The interview was horrendous. Victoria made her feel small and useless, but eventually she gave her a trial, simply through utter desperation, as her last second assistant had walked out without notice.

She worked with someone named Louise. Louise was the first assistant and never let Holly forget that. Between Victoria and Louise, she was miserable. There were tales of how awful her job was and how much she hated Victoria.

The entries became less frequent. When she did write, it was to vent her anguish at her job and her relationship.

Eventually, Holly had done something right. She was trusted with the keys to Victoria's house and the duties of waiting late each night for the Book to be prepared. She'd then deliver the Book to Victoria's house, hoping that she never bumped into the woman as she did.

The extra hours in the office allowed her more time to write in her journal, but the entries were difficult to stomach. Victoria was a monster to her second assistant and nothing Holly did was good enough.

In a few short weeks, Holly had adapted everything about herself in order to try to fit in. Her clothes, her hair, her makeup, and her attitude all changed in an attempt to appease Victoria. But nothing worked.

Respite came in the form of a new friend, Gideon. He was a lifeline and seemingly the only sane person at *Arrival*. He helped Holly to change her outfits so that they suited her style and wouldn't offend Victoria's delicate sensibilities. He explained the business and soothed her emotions when Victoria had been overly harsh.

Then one night, Holly was waiting for the Book alone in the office. It was the anniversary of her parents' death, a date that always cast a long shadow over her day. Victoria glided into the office, returning from dinner with one of the lead advertisers. She stopped in front of Holly's desk and said in an impossibly quiet voice, "I know it's none of my business, but I am truly sorry for your loss." And then she sent Holly home early.

She had no idea how Victoria knew, she wondered if Gideon had given her a heads-up. It heralded the first time that Victoria had been a human being to her. The event truly affected Holly, and she started to analyse Victoria's words and behaviours in more detail. Now that she suspected that Victoria had a heart underneath the ice, she looked more critically at her boss' actions. With a little detective work, she realised that Victoria's dragon persona was mainly an act.

Holly began to see why Victoria acted the way she did. She understood that Victoria wasn't demanding a schedule change just to be awkward, she was trying to get home to Alexia who was sick. She didn't fire the wardrobe manager on a whim, he'd been harassing a model who was too frightened to make an official complaint. She didn't want the latest must-have Apple accessory to prove she could get it before release, she wanted it to apologise to Hugo for being so absent during his exams.

The mask remained. To everyone else, Victoria was being her usual self. But Holly knew better. The one act of kindness had caused her to understand Victoria had a good heart and she was determined to not let Victoria push her away. She'd be the best assistant she could be.

By the end of the journal it was very clear that Holly's opinion of Victoria had fundamentally changed, even if Victoria was as rude as ever. Journal Holly waited for the day when she would finally break through the dragon's thick skin.

In the here and now, she picked up the next journal.

She knew how this one ended and was fascinated to know how she got there. A few pages in, it seemed that Kate's career wasn't going as well as she'd hoped. She wasn't progressing, and she was miserable. Now she wanted to go back to culinary school. Moreover, she wanted Holly to get a better job so she could support the both of them while Kate trained.

Holly refused to leave Victoria. She never referred to her job as working at *Arrival*, it was always working for Victoria. Kate pushed hard for Holly to leave. They fought constantly. Her home life was in turmoil, but every morning she'd go into work and feel relieved that Victoria was there, being herself. A stabilising force in her life.

Victoria may have been mean, but she was driven, focused, wise, and strong. There were moments when she would turn to Holly and tell her that she needed to be more assertive, or hand her responsibility for a meeting. In her own strange way, she was telling Holly that she trusted her. She was helping Holly to become more.

Holly smiled as she read about herself coming to a realisation. She'd seen it coming. But it hit her former self like a brick wall. She was in love. Or, at the very least, in lust. In… *something* with her terrifying boss.

The diary entry that made the proclamation rambled on for four long pages. She seemed to wrestle with the idea. At one point, she wondered if she was suffering from Stockholm syndrome, or simply in awe of the power that the editor held. But no, by the end of the declaration, she had decided that it was love.

Holly closed her eyes to take it all in. Condensing so

much of her life into such a short amount of time was a lot to take in one sitting.

The Victoria in the book and the woman she knew now seemed like completely different people. Her former self would have been euphoric to see her boss as Holly had been introduced to her. In many ways, Holly realised that her former self was right. There was a whole other person behind the mask. And now she was lucky enough to see that other person, the real Victoria Hastings. She wished she could go back in time and tell herself that she'd been right all along.

"Holly?"

Her eyes snapped open. Victoria stood by the door. Holly clapped the journal shut.

"H-hi, sorry, I didn't hear you," Holly said.

"Well, I practically shouted myself hoarse," Victoria muttered.

Holly smiled. She knew that Victoria had probably only called her a couple of times in her soft voice.

"Sorry," she repeated.

"I have spoken with Gideon. He would like to come for brunch tomorrow. If that is suitable?"

"Absolutely, I'm looking forward to meeting him."

Victoria glanced with hesitation at the diaries. Holly knew that she must be dying of curiosity, but she didn't want to get into that conversation. There was too much damning evidence inside the leather-bound tomes.

"And my children will be home tomorrow afternoon. They are aware of the situation and they understand. Well, as much as a fourteen- and eight-year-old can understand."

"I look forward to meeting them, too," Holly said. It

was true. She was very curious to know more about the children.

"Very well, I'll leave you to it." Victoria left the room.

Holly waited until she heard Victoria get to the top of the stairs before picking up the journal again. She was eager to read more. She needed to find out exactly what she had said and done, if anything, about her growing feelings for Victoria.

In the back of her mind she wondered if anything had ever happened. There was a slim chance that something had, and now Victoria was pretending it hadn't. But Holly didn't think that was something Victoria would do.

She took a slow, deep breath before reopening the journal. She had a lot of catching up to do.

CHAPTER TWENTY-NINE

Victoria swirled her teaspoon around the cooling liquid in the cup. It was a couple of hours until Gideon was due to come for brunch, and she was already dreading it.

Holly knew everything. That much was clear. She could feel the younger woman slipping away.

Ever since they went to the damned storage unit and found those blasted journals, Holly had been squirreled away in the basement guestroom. She didn't even come upstairs for lunch, despite previously saying that she had been hungry.

Eventually Victoria had gone down under the guise of telling her that Gideon had called about brunch the next day. He hadn't. It was an excuse to see Holly and figure out what was going on. It was fruitless, and she had to call Gideon and order him to come over for brunch regardless of any existing plans.

The girl didn't show up for dinner either. Eventually Victoria took a sandwich downstairs. Holly must have read all about what an evil monster she was. That explained why she was hiding in the safety of her room. Regardless, Victoria wasn't about to let her starve.

During the two brief occasions she ventured downstairs, Holly gave little away. She was pleasant. She smiled. But nothing else. Said nothing of the contents of the diaries. Nothing of when she would be leaving. Because, of course, she must be planning her immediate escape.

Victoria tried to focus her attention on the newspaper in front of her. Just because things were again falling apart, it didn't mean she wouldn't keep up her usual breakfast routine.

Out of the corner of her eye, she saw Holly enter the kitchen.

Victoria raised an eyebrow. "Ah, she returns," she said without feeling.

"Yes, I'm back," Holly said. "Still getting caught up. But those journals are amazing. I'm learning so much about, well, me."

Victoria hummed in agreement. She saw Holly making herself some tea and returned to her newspaper. A thick atmosphere clung to the room. She didn't know what to say, nor did she have any intention of being the one to break the silence.

After a while, she realised that she felt watched. She glanced up and saw Holly had been looking at her. Holly looked away, a blush appearing on her cheeks as she did.

Victoria angrily returned to her newspaper. No doubt Holly was remembering some terrible thing she'd said or done. Presumably wondering when the evil dragon would be making a reappearance. The next few hours or days were going to be unbearable.

By the time the doorbell rang to signal Gideon's arrival, both women heaved a silent sigh of relief. Holly had no idea what she had done to offend Victoria, but the woman was definitely doing her best to avoid speaking to her. Holly was looking forward to the presence of a third person to try to put the day back on track.

Victoria opened the front door while Holly stood by the stairway anxiously. Gideon was a tall man with a bald head and glasses. He was impeccable dressed in a three-piece suit, and Holly suddenly felt underdressed.

Victoria and Gideon said hello and air-kissed in greeting. Gideon held two red roses, one of which he handed to Victoria as he stepped into the hallway.

He noticed Holly standing shyly in the corner and smiled warmly.

"Well, let me look at you," he said excitedly.

Holly approached him. She felt nervous but excited. Gideon was another piece of the puzzle that was her previous life, and she was anxious to find out more about him.

Gideon looked at Victoria with a smile. "She's as gorgeous as ever, isn't she?"

Victoria smiled politely but remained silent. She was looking from Gideon to Holly, presumably wondering if Holly would remember him.

Gideon turned back to Holly. "You have no idea who I am, do you?" he said with a jovial grin.

"No, I'm sorry… there's nothing," Holly apologised.

"Well, in that case we simply have to talk about the

hundred dollars that you owe me." He winked and handed her the other rose.

Holly accepted the rose and laughed. "Oh, I see! That's why you were so keen to see me."

They shared a laugh. Victoria smiled but didn't make a move to join them, holding back and giving them space.

"Well, the first thing that you need to know about me is that I'm a hugger." He held his arms open.

Holly beamed with happiness. She, too, was a hugger. Not that there had been much opportunity for human contact over recent months.

They hugged, and when she stepped back, he looked her up and down with appreciation.

"You're looking divine, if a little underweight," he told her. "I'm loving the hair."

"Thanks, I've seen some photographs of myself with long hair now. I'm wondering if I should grow it long or keep it like this."

"One of the last things you said to me was that you were looking for the new you," Gideon said. "I think maybe the shorter hair is the new you."

"Yes!" Holly said with excitement. "I was reading my journal and I mentioned that conversation I had with you. We were at that club… where was it?"

"Bar 29." Gideon smiled. "But hold on, a journal? This sounds intriguing."

"Bar 29, that was it. And, yeah. I seem to have written down everything that's ever happened to me."

"Bet you didn't write anything down about that hundred dollars." He laughed.

Holly cocked her head to one side, pretending to search her memory. "No, still not ringing any bells."

"If you'll excuse me," Victoria said as she glided past them, "I will prepare brunch. Please use the sitting room upstairs to get reacquainted. It's not Bar 29, but I'm sure it will do."

Once the older woman had vanished into the kitchen, Gideon turned and looked at her with a raised eyebrow.

"Oh dear," he muttered.

"Yeah, that's my fault." Holly sighed. "It's been weird lately."

Gideon put his arm around her and guided her towards the stairs. "Oh, honey, it's always been weird..."

Brunch was awkward. Holly immediately felt an affinity for Gideon, but, while they laughed and joked, Victoria remained silent. Each time Holly tried to include Victoria in the conversation, she was shot down with a sarcastic comment or a scathing remark. Usually followed by an apology and an insistence that she was simply tired.

Eventually, Victoria excused herself from the dining room, saying there was an urgent call that needed to be made.

As soon as she was gone, and the study door was closed, Holly turned to face Gideon.

"Gideon, can I ask you something?"

Gideon leaned on his hand and looked at her with a grin. "Yes?"

"I get the feeling we were close. I know from my journal

that we were friends, but… I need to know; did I confide in you?"

"Like what?" Gideon looked like he was playing dumb. He was clearly enjoying Holly's discomfort. She had to smile, he was just the kind of friend she'd be attracted to.

"Anything I need to know about," Holly pressed.

"Such as?" Gideon picked up a scone and cut it in half.

The ball was in her court. If she wanted an answer, she'd have to ask the question.

"Did I ever mention my feelings for Victoria?"

Gideon didn't look surprised by the admission. He shook his head. "Not directly, no. But I certainly had my suspicions."

Holly nodded and stared into her empty teacup. She'd hoped that she might have confided in Gideon, that he might be able to offer her some guidance.

"Is that what's going on here?" He indicated Victoria's empty chair with his knife, then dipped it into the butter dish.

"No, nothing like that. I'm not sure what it's about to be honest."

"I see." He buttered his scone. "So, what do you propose to do about it?"

"About what?"

"Your feelings for Victoria."

"Shh!" Holly cried out. She craned her neck towards the closed door to the hallway, in case Victoria was there.

Gideon laughed. "Come on, where's the brave Holly I know and love? Hm? The one who was starting a brave new life. I don't want to downplay what happened to you, please don't think that, but this could be a gift. A rewrite, a clean slate. What happened to the girl who didn't want to waste another second?"

"I did say that, didn't I?"

"You did. You were so miserable with Kate that when you finally decided to make the break, you wanted to become a new person. To retake control of your life. You had big plans."

"I did. I do. I still do," Holly admitted. "I read those entries in my journal. My relationship was falling apart, the only stability I had was *Arrival*. Well, Victoria. Even though she was awful to me."

"How has she been now?"

Holly smiled. "Wonderful. Well, moody, too. But she has been there for me through everything, dealt with everything. The guestroom, oh my god, Gideon, I never want to leave. It's like heaven. She's thought of everything. Even if she doesn't want to admit it or make a big deal of it."

"So, considering what you read in your journal and what you have seen now... what do you think?"

"That Victoria has lost her mind?"

"Maybe." Gideon chuckled. "But let's suppose she hasn't. Let's suppose she is actually being nice to you. Building a friendship. Why would she do that?"

Holly opened and closed her mouth. "No... I know what you're thinking, but I can't... I can't take that risk. Maybe she's just being nice."

"Of course, yes, she's well-known for her kind deeds."

Holly stared at him. "Do you *know* something?"

"I know lots of things."

"Anything relevant to my current situation?" Holly asked.

Gideon sighed. He lowered his scone to the plate and steepled his fingers. He looked at her seriously. "Holly, I would never break a confidence. I wouldn't tell Victoria anything you told me, or even anything I suspected. Likewise, I wouldn't tell you if Victoria had told me anything. Even if it would be ever so relevant to your current situation," he emphasised.

Holly felt her mouth run dry. He knew something. She wanted to reach across the table and grab him by the collar and force him to spill whatever secrets he knew.

"Victoria is surprisingly nervous when it comes to matters of the heart," Gideon continued. "In all the years I've known her, she's never been comfortable with the thought of anyone loving her. The confidence, the bravado, is all fake. She is so keen to protect herself that she often pushes people away."

Holly held her breath, silently begging Gideon to continue. Any insight she could get would be welcome.

"She also often makes assumptions," Gideon said meaningfully.

"Assumptions?" Holly asked.

"Yes. Think of your most negative view of a situation, that's Victoria's default position. And with that, I should stop talking. I consider her one of my dearest friends, but I know she'd happily bus me down to the mail room if she heard me talking about her like this."

Holly understood. Victoria seemed to be a knee-jerk reaction kind of person.

Gideon looked at his watch and sighed. "Sadly, I have to leave. But I want to see you again soon, if you're agreeable?"

"Absolutely, you feel familiar to me, and it's so nice to be able to talk to someone."

They shared contact details, and Holly gave him a farewell hug. Gideon stepped into Victoria's office to say goodbye before he left.

Holly cleared away the brunch things before returning to the guestroom to immerse herself in more journals and to process what Gideon had said. She wondered if it could be possible that Victoria had feelings for her, too. It didn't seem likely with the foul mood Victoria had been in.

But Gideon was hinting at something. She wondered what he meant by alluding to Victoria making assumptions. Was he suggesting that she had made an assumption? If so, what was it?

She decided that she needed to spend more time with Victoria to get an idea what the older woman was feeling. Victoria certainly wasn't going to come to her, so she needed to make the first move.

CHAPTER THIRTY

It was an hour after Gideon left that Holly finally plucked up the courage to knock on the closed door of Victoria's study.

"Come," Victoria replied tersely.

Holly took a deep breath and opened the door.

She walked in and noted Victoria at her desk, hunched over the Arrival Book. Victoria didn't look up. Holly sat on the sofa and waited silently. She knew Victoria would have to at least acknowledge her presence.

It took a few long, icy minutes before Victoria raised her head and steely green eyes looked at her questioningly.

"I need to talk to you," Holly said.

Victoria sighed. She lowered her pen and took off her glasses. "You do?"

"Yes, if you're not too busy?"

"It depends on what you're here to say."

"You're not making this very easy," Holly grumbled.

"Well, I'm not sure I wish to hear it." Victoria laughed half-heartedly.

"What? Why?"

"I presume this is about your journals?" Victoria asked. "You've come to tell me you wish to leave?"

Holly blinked. Was this what Victoria's mood had been about?

"I can just imagine the contents of your journals," Victoria continued. "I made your life a living hell, I'm sure. So, if you're here to tell me just how awful I was—"

"No," Holly interrupted. "Not at all."

Victoria looked cynical. "No?"

"No. And I don't want to leave, unless you want me to go? I don't want to overstay my welcome."

Victoria's jaw clenched. She shook her head. "I don't want you to leave, this is your home for as long as you want it to be."

Holly smiled. "Good, because I love being here. I love getting to know you better."

Victoria snorted a laugh. "Oh, I'm sure everything you need to know is in your journals. Maybe you haven't read that part yet?"

"I've read everything I'd written about my work at *Arrival*," Holly admitted. "I liked and admired you then, and I feel the same way now."

Victoria's eyes snapped up in shock.

"I wanted to say that I'm sorry if I've upset you in some way," Holly dove into her prepared speech. "You've been distant, and I haven't liked it, especially if it's in any way my fault. So, if I've done something, then please accept this as a blanket apology. But maybe you're just tired like you said you were. In which case, maybe there's something I can do to help? I feel a bit useless anyway, and if I can… assist in some way, that would be cool."

Holly knew it was important to provide Victoria with an out. It was obvious that she was upset, but it was also obvious that she wouldn't want to make a big deal of it. Or probably even acknowledge it. Giving her the option to cover it over with tiredness was best for everyone.

Victoria swallowed and then coughed lightly. "Um, well, you have nothing to a-apologise for." She sat up a little straighter. "As I said before, I'm tired, just… tired."

Holly knew it was a lie, but she was willing to allow Victoria the space. Especially now that they were actually talking.

"How can I help?" Holly was already on her feet and pulling over a chair from against the wall to place it in front of Victoria's desk. "Really, anything. I'll hold a paperclip if you like."

Victoria looked at a loss for a moment. She looked down at the Book on her desk.

"Could you look for an old issue for me? I think it was September or October 2010? I'm sure I've seen a similar headline to this before." She tapped her finger on an article.

"Sure!" Holly turned to the bookcase she had looked at the previous evening and searched for the edition. She was glad to have her back to Victoria as a wide smile covered her face.

CHAPTER THIRTY-ONE

Victoria and her children had a tradition. Whenever they returned from a trip without her, she would pick them up herself at the airport or train station personally. It was her gesture to remind them how much she loved them, even though she had to send them away on occasion because of her work.

After hugs were exchanged, they always went for ice cream. In recent years, it had become frozen yoghurt, which was much healthier. The children would have giant cups of frozen yoghurt with whatever toppings they liked, as long as one was fruit. And occasionally, Victoria would steal a bit or two.

Alexia loved the tradition. At eight, she was still at an age where her forgiveness could be bought with a sugary treat. Hugo was fifteen and sometimes harder to appease.

"So, Holly's in the guestroom?" Alexia asked before taking another bite of her strawberry frozen yoghurt.

"No, I put her in your room. You're in Izzy's bed." Victoria took a swipe of Alexia's yoghurt.

"Mom!" Alexia laughed.

"Of course she's in the guestroom," Hugo said. He rolled his eyes in a way that Victoria knew mirrored her own.

"I thought she might be in Dad's old room," Alexia defended.

"Why would she be in there?" Victoria frowned.

"In case you needed to keep an eye on her. Because of her memory and stuff."

"I see. No, she's in the guestroom. She's doing well, she just doesn't have all of her memories yet."

"But she'll remember us, won't she?" Alexia asked.

"No," Hugo glowered, "why would she remember us, stupid?"

"Hugo, be nice," Victoria warned.

He grumbled an apology to his sister.

"I don't understand how she can forget everything. How does that happen?" Alexia asked.

"It's very complicated," Victoria said softly. "The brain is a very complicated part of the body. We don't properly understand it yet. Sometimes things happen to the brain and we don't know why. But, in answer to your question, no, Holly won't remember you."

"But she'll remember us after she's met us again, right?" Alexia asked. "Like, will she forget us again? Will we have to tell her who we are every morning?"

Victoria smiled. "No, sweetheart, she remembers everything that has happened after the accident. She just can't remember anything before it."

"Does anyone know what happened to her?" Hugo

asked. He toyed his spoon around his chocolate frozen yoghurt.

"Unfortunately not," Victoria said. She used her spoon to swipe a bit of chocolate brownie from his cup.

"Sounds scary," Alexia said.

"It was, which is why we have to be the best hosts we can. We must make her feel at home and safe and welcome."

"Why is she staying with us?" Hugo asked.

"Because she doesn't have anyone else," Victoria answered

Hugo stopped moving his spoon and looked up at his mother. "Like, no one?"

"No one."

He raised an eyebrow and returned his attention to his treat.

"Can we go down to the guestroom and see her?" Alexia asked. "Because the more time she spends with us, the more she might remember us. And then she might remember other things."

Victoria smiled at her daughter's innocent simplicity. "I see your thinking, but it's unlikely that her memories will come back that way. She may never remember. So we need to focus on making good memories rather than trying to bring back old ones."

"Has she remembered anything?" Hugo asked.

Victoria resisted the urge to mention that Holly recalled the damn dog, although she'd have to eventually. She shook her head. "Nothing specific as far as I'm aware. She says she feels sensations, like a faint memory of knowing something or feeling something. But nothing too specific."

"But we can go and see her, right?" Alexia pushed.

"Of course, sweetheart, but you must respect her privacy. Like you would any other guest. Although I would hope that she will spend most of her time with us in the main part of the house."

"I wonder if she'll remember how to play Xbox with us," Hugo mused.

Victoria felt her jaw slacken. "Pardon?"

Hugo looked up at her. "Holly used to play Xbox with us, some of the Lego games mainly. When you were running late."

Victoria's mind spun. She had no idea that her children had ever socialised with Holly. She knew that Holly had run errands which involved them, had met them, had spoken to them. But this seemed to be something more.

"Did this happen often?"

"Yeah, a few times," Hugo said unhelpfully.

"I see."

"Is she in trouble?" Alexia asked sadly.

"No, no… not in trouble. I just didn't know."

"We didn't say because Holly was cool and you'd probably fire her if you knew," Alexia offered.

"Shh." Hugo shoved his sister gently. "It was fine, Mom. We made her come upstairs and play, she didn't want to."

Victoria nodded. "I understand. It hardly matters now. I just… didn't know."

"Can she play with us now?" Alexia asked.

"If she wants to, I'm not her keeper." Victoria shrugged.

"You kind of are," Hugo pointed out.

"Eat your yoghurt before it melts," Victoria said. She wasn't about to have this conversation. She didn't need

Alexia asking a million awkward questions about power of attorney rights, a detail she'd only shared with Hugo over the phone.

"What do you mean?" Alexia asked.

"Eat your yoghurt as well," Victoria said. "We need to head home soon."

Alexia knew it was time to stop asking questions and wisely got on with eating. Hugo continued to look at her with a raised eyebrow and a smirk on his face. She glared at him. He chuckled and looked down at his chocolaty treat. Sadly, the glare had stopped working on him many years before. She hoped he wouldn't prove to be too much trouble over the coming days.

CHAPTER THIRTY-TWO

Holly heard the front door opening and the murmuring of conversation. She sucked in a deep breath and put a smile on her face as she walked out of the study and into the hallway.

"Holly!" Alexia ran towards her and pulled her into a hug.

Holly was surprised by the reaction. She knew from her journals that she looked after the kids once or twice, but she had no idea that Alexia was so fond of her.

"Hey," Holly greeted.

Victoria had a shocked expression on her face, too.

"Hey Holly," Hugo said. "Cool hair."

"Thanks," Holly smiled.

"Yeah, really cool hair," Alexia said as she stood back and gazed up at Holly in awe. "Holly, will you watch a movie with me tonight?"

"Alexia," Victoria said in a warning tone.

"It's fine," Holly reassured her. She loved how friendly

Alexia was, it felt so good to have someone look up to her. "Absolutely, but remember you have school tomorrow."

Alexia's face became serious. "Do you not remember me at all?"

Holly bit her lip and shook her head sadly. "No, I'm sorry, honey."

"Do you remember Hugo?" Alexia asked.

"Of course she doesn't," Hugo said. He rolled his eyes and picked up his suitcase from where the driver had left it by the door.

"I'm sorry, I don't remember anyone," Holly said.

"But—"

"Alexia…" Victoria warned again.

"It's fine, Victoria." She looked down at Alexia. "I don't remember anyone. But that doesn't mean that we can't hang out and have fun like we used to. Maybe my memories will come back one day, maybe they won't. I'm okay with that."

"Mom said you remembered Izzy," Alexia pointed out.

Holly looked up at Victoria who was looking more and more uncomfortable.

"Well, erm, yes, I did. I had a flashback, of sorts…"

"Like in the movies?" Alexia asked.

"Was there a flash of light when you remembered?" Hugo asked. He was on the first step of the staircase, but the news of a potential flashback had him interested.

"No, unfortunately it wasn't that dramatic," Holly deadpanned.

"What about banging you on the head again?" Alexia asked. "Has anyone tried banging you on the head?"

"No one is hitting Holly on the head. Now, both of you

go to your rooms and unpack." Victoria said sternly. It was clear the conversation was over.

"Fine," Alexia said.

"We'll talk later," Hugo said. He started to climb the stairs.

"I still think you should talk to your doctor about it," Alexia grumbled quietly.

"I'll be sure to mention it," Holly agreed. She walked over to Alexia's suitcase. "Come on, I'll help you unpack."

"Holly, do you want to play on the Xbox? I could set it up, if you like," Hugo called down the stairs. "I mean, you used to play. Maybe you'll remember something?"

"Sounds great," Holly said.

"Yay!" Alexia cheered. "I'm so glad you're back, Holly. You're so cool."

Alexia picked up her suitcase and handed Holly her backpack. The young girl ran up the stairs.

Holly turned to Victoria and smiled. "I'm cool."

"Oh, shut up." Victoria grinned.

"And my hair… is *really cool*," Holly added.

"Go away. Play your game." Victoria shooed her away with her hands, but the smile remained on her face.

"Mom said we can have pizza!" Alexia announced.

Hugo paused the game they were playing and turned around to look at his sister in astonishment.

"Mom said we can have pizza? Like… our mom?" he asked.

"Yep." Alexia placed the glass of juice she had gone to get on the coffee table and sat on the sofa.

Holly looked from Alexia to Hugo. "I take it that's unusual?"

"She said we can eat it in here," Alexia added.

Holly thought that Hugo's eyes were going to fall out of his head.

"Seriously? Are you joking with us?" he demanded.

"Seriously. She was working and I asked her what we were doing for dinner and she gave me this." Alexia produced a black credit card from her back pocket. "She said we can order pizza and eat it in here. She said the smell of the pizza would make her ill so she's going to eat on her own."

Hugo dropped the controller to the floor. "I'm gonna speak to her."

"You don't believe me?" Alexia asked.

"Nope."

Holly laughed. "Is it that unusual that she'd let you do this?"

Hugo nodded his head seriously. "Yeah. Like, alien abduction unusual. I'll be back in a minute. Don't touch the game."

"I wouldn't dare, I'm beating you," Holly said with a smirk. It hadn't taken her long to discover that she was good at video games.

"For now." Hugo grinned. He left the games room in search of his mother.

"You're going to be in big trouble if you're lying," Holly nudged Alexia softly.

"I'm not lying," Alexia said. "Mom's in a weird mood. I

asked if she wanted to come up and play, but she said she didn't want to get in the way."

"I hope you told her she wouldn't be in the way," Holly pressed.

Alexia nodded quickly. "I did. But that's when she said we were having pizza and the smell makes her sick."

Holly wasn't so sure that was the truth of the matter, but she also didn't want to discuss it with Victoria's eight-year-old daughter.

"Mom really missed you when you were gone, she didn't say anything, but it was obvious to me," Alexia said.

"I bet she had a lot of work to do without a good second assistant," Holly agreed.

"It was more than that. Mom liked you. You made her happy."

Holly laughed heartily. "I doubt that. Maybe I made her life easier and that made her happy."

Alexia shook her head. "No, that wasn't it. I hope you stay."

"Stay?" Holly asked.

"Yeah, stay with us. For a while at least. Mom might be grumpy sometimes, but that's just how she is when she's nervous. She probably doesn't want you seeing that she's nice. Because you were her assistant and she had to be strict and stuff."

Holly thought that Alexia's childlike analysis was fairly spot on.

"Well, I *know* that your mom is nice," Holly admitted. "I know she hides it."

"Were you friends?"

"Well, no… no. But I knew. I worked closely with her,

so I knew her well." Holly cringed at how that sounded. Especially knowing the secrets that lurked in her journals.

"Maybe you can be friends now?"

"Maybe," Holly agreed. *If friends draw erotic pictures of each other,* she thought.

"Why are you blushing?" Alexia asked, her head cocked to the side in curiosity.

Holly felt her cheeks heating up. The slight blush was becoming a full-on fire now that Alexia had pointed it out. She didn't know what to say. Her blush was getting more and more out of control, and her brain wasn't providing her with any words.

"You like her!" Alexia whispered, her mouth and eyes opening in shock.

Holly put down her game controller and leaned towards Alexia and shushed her.

"You do, you like Mom!" Alexia said a little louder as her excitement grew.

"Alexia, please, you have to be quiet. You know what your mom's like, she'll get embarrassed and then she'll get mad."

Alexia nodded. She turned to look at the open door onto the upstairs landing. She quickly jumped over the back of the sofa and slammed the door closed. She rushed back and stood in front of Holly, clapping her hands with excitement.

"So, she doesn't know?"

Holly debated denying everything, but she suspected that Alexia wouldn't believe her. She seemed to be as detail-oriented as her mother, she'd seen right through her. Denial would simply stoke Alexia's curiosity. Admission would help to bond them, and therefore help her keep control over the situation.

"No, and I'd prefer if she didn't," Holly said firmly.

Alexia frowned. "Why not? If she doesn't know, then you'll never be together. You want to be together, don't you?"

Holly let out a frustrated sigh. She took Alexia's arms and gestured for the girl to take the seat beside her.

"Sometimes, it's hard for adults to be honest with each other. Especially with stuff like this. Your mom, she doesn't exactly wear her heart on her sleeve. And she gets embarrassed easily, and then she gets angry. I don't want her to feel uncomfortable in her own house. Do you see what I mean? I think it's best to keep things quiet. Does that make sense?"

Alexia nodded. "Yeah, I understand. You're a coward."

Holly blinked. Suddenly she remembered that this was Victoria Hastings daughter in front of her.

"No, well… I…"

"No, you're a coward," Alexia repeated. "You obviously have feelings for Mom, but you don't want to say anything in case it goes wrong."

Holly opened her mouth to refute the claim but found she couldn't. Alexia was right.

"I won't say anything, don't worry," Alexia promised. "If you want to be sad all your life, then that's up to you."

"Low blow," Holly mumbled.

"But I could help you, if you wanted," Alexia pressed.

Holly narrowed her eyes. This girl was already a master manipulator and negotiator. Victoria would be proud.

"Help me how?"

"I could give you advice. I won't say anything because

then Mom would really be mad. But I could tell you what to say, or what to do. I know her favourite food, chocolates, flowers."

"You'd do that?"

"Of course! You did make Mom happy before, even if you don't think so. After you left, she got really sad for a long time."

Holly's heart clenched at the thought of her disappearance upsetting Victoria. The last thing she wanted to do was hurt her again. She tried to look as stern and serious as possible as she turned to look at Alexia.

"Alexia, look… I… I do like your mom. A lot. And maybe she likes me. But I need you to know that sometimes things just don't work out. I don't want you to think that this will, because it might not. And me and your mom…" Holly let out a sigh. "It's practically impossible. We're from different worlds, there's the age gap, you guys, my illness. I'm just saying, don't be upset if nothing happens, okay?"

Alexia nodded. "Holly, my mom and dad got divorced when I was six, it's fine. I'm not a baby."

Holly grinned to herself. "Gotcha."

"So, Mom totally won't make the first move. And she won't notice unless your moves are, like, really obvious."

Holly wasn't sure if taking dating advice from an eight-year-old was the best idea, but she didn't have any of her own. And if anyone was going to have advice on wooing Victoria Hastings, it was the girl on front of her.

"Okay. Hit me," Holly said.

Alexia gave her an appraising look. "Maybe you should be writing this down?" she suggested.

CHAPTER THIRTY-THREE

VICTORIA CLOSED her eyes and leaned her head against the leather headrest of the limousine. Monday had been a relief. As usual, it was full of incompetence and she'd been tempted to fire two associate editors, but at least she had been out of the house.

She just didn't know whether she was coming or going at the moment. One minute she was miserable that Holly had remembered the dog and not her, but then she spent hours working with Holly by her side and she felt whole again. But soon after, the girl was locked away in the games room with the children, trying to escape from her once again.

It was obvious what was happening. Holly was caught in a precarious position between feeling gratitude for Victoria rescuing her from France and coming to the realisation that Victoria was the devil in heels. Holly must not want to upset her, especially considering she held power of attorney over her, was responsible for her medical attention, her food, her shelter. Of course Holly was trying to keep the peace.

Now it was up to Victoria to do the same.

It didn't help that her ludicrous dreams were keeping her awake night after night. Looking Holly in the eye was becoming a challenge. Luckily, she had the excuse of work. She was perfectly happy to lock herself away in her study and give Holly the run on the house. It meant she didn't have any fodder for new dreams. And it gave Holly a break from the charm offensive she'd been on to try to convince Victoria that everything was fine and well.

The car pulled up to the kerb, and her heart started to sink. Being depressed at arriving home wasn't a new feeling for her. In the past, it had been thanks to her ex-husband. Now it was a charming, beautiful, and caring young woman whose life she had destroyed. *This too shall pass*, she reminded herself.

Her driver opened the door, and she stepped out.

"Thank you, Charles."

"Good night, Miss Hastings."

She walked up the short flight of steps and unlocked the door.

Hugo stood in the hallway with a bottle of water in his hand and a shocked expression on his face.

She closed the door behind her. "Something wrong, sweetheart?"

He looked at his watch. "It's five thirty."

"Yes?" She hung her coat in the closet.

"You're never home this early."

"It's not the first time I've been home on time," she pointed out.

"First time this year," he argued.

She was about to deny it when she realised that she wasn't sure. She often worked late, and one week turned into another and suddenly months had flown by. He did look positively stunned to see her there. Maybe it had been that long.

"Well, I'm here now. How are you? How was school?"

"What do you care?" He started to walk towards the stairs.

"Now hold on," Victoria called after him. "What's that supposed to mean?"

He stood on the first step and turned to face her. It was only now that she realised he looked upset. His cheeks glowed, and she wondered if he had been crying.

"You haven't asked me how school was for…" He paused and laughed. "I can't even remember when."

"That's simply not true." Now she was sure he was wrong. She made sure to keep up to date with her children's schooling. No matter the cost to her own work schedule, she was at every parent-teacher meeting.

"School was fine." He turned on his heel to go up the stairs.

"Hugo, don't turn your back on me."

"I don't feel well. I'm going to sleep, I'll eat dinner later." He continued up the stairs and then up the next flight before slamming his bedroom door shut.

She clenched and unclenched her fists. She wanted to march up the stairs and demand to know where her sweet boy had gone. He never spoke to her like that. But she knew that it was no use chasing after him. He needed to cool down and come to her. The realisation didn't make it any easier.

She heard giggling and leaned over the bannister. Holly and Alexia were down in the guestroom. She stood up straight and pinched the bridge of her nose.

Something bumped into her, and she turned around to see Izzy looking at her with big, sad eyes. Admittedly she had been ignoring the beast since the initial incident with Holly.

"Yes, yes, I see you," she mumbled.

Izzy whimpered.

"And I'm sorry." She reached a hand down and scratched at the dog's ear. "I'm sorry."

"Mom? Is that you?" Alexia called from downstairs.

"Yes, sweetheart," she called back.

Alexia launched herself up the stairs and pulled her into a hug. "You're home early."

She closed her eyes and held onto her daughter tightly. This was the greeting she had expected, though maybe not deserved.

"Holly and I are going to cook dinner," Alexia said.

She opened her eyes and saw Holly smiling at her.

"I see, and what feast are we having?"

"Pizza," Holly said with a mischievous grin.

"Oh, really?" Victoria narrowed her eyes at the blatant teasing.

"Tuna steaks and couscous," Alexia said.

Victoria felt her stomach rumble at the thought of her favourite meal.

"A little bird tells me you like it," Holly said. The girl leaned on the bannister rail and winked at her.

"Um. Yes… I do." She turned to Alexia. "What's wrong with your brother?"

Alexia shrugged. "I don't know, he's been moody since we got home."

"Did something happen at school?"

"I don't know, he doesn't talk to me."

"Nor me, it seems," Victoria said.

"I'm sure he'll come around. We'll make him some food, hopefully that will cheer him up," Holly said.

"Maybe so." She glanced up the stairs, still wondering if she should go after her son.

Alexia took her arm. "Come on, Mom. Come and sit in the kitchen with us."

She found herself dragged into the kitchen and deposited on a stool at the breakfast bar.

"Isn't it cool that Holly knows how to cook your favourite meal?"

"It is," Victoria agreed.

She looked at Holly who was making eye contact with her. She didn't know if she was imagining it, but it looked like Holly was wearing extra makeup. She was also wearing the low-cut, Donna Karan cowl-neck cashmere top that Victoria had asked to have put in her wardrobe. She always thought the cut would suit the girl. She was right. Now she was struggling to ensure she didn't look. Her overactive imagination didn't need to add that to the repertoire.

"Want to be my sous chef?" Holly asked. "Or do you want to watch?"

It sounded awfully suggestive, and Victoria's eyes flicked to Alexia who was putting on an apron.

"I… have some emails to answer." She got her phone

out of her handbag. It wasn't a lie. Leaving early did mean a backlog of work would have accumulated.

As she checked her phone she could feel eyes resting heavily on her. It was going to be a long evening.

Holly sat on the sofa in the games room and stared blankly at the television. She normally loved *Groundhog Day* and would laugh all the way through it. This time the jokes seemed stale and overthought. She turned to watch Alexia who sat in the middle spot of the sofa. The young girl laughed and laughed, tugging on either Holly's or her brother's arms to ensure they were catching every second of her favourite film.

"Yeah, I heard it," Hugo muttered at Alexia's latest insistent pull on his arm.

Like Holly, he wasn't enjoying himself. He flopped on the other end of the sofa, his long legs resting on the coffee table. He'd had his phone in his hand and had been glumly scrolling through it since Holly and Alexia came into the room. He hadn't joined them for dinner, but Victoria had prepared a plate that Alexia had taken up to him.

Holly let out a sigh and turned her head back to the television. She wished relationships were as predictable as they were on film. Alexia had sworn faithfully that Victoria liked her. And yet, over dinner preparation and dinner itself, Victoria steadfastly ignored her. Holly upped the ante a few times with some risqué comments and some blatant flirting. Victoria had looked confused before turning her attention to something else.

In the end, Holly had stopped trying. She feared Victoria would decide she was suffering some latent effects from her accident and would have her admitted to the hospital at once.

After dinner, Victoria had disappeared into her study. Holly was convinced she was avoiding her. Alexia suggested it was more likely she was avoiding Hugo. Now Holly suspected she was avoiding them both.

The movie was paused, and Alexia jumped to her feet. "I'm going to ask Mom if I can have popcorn!"

"Careful," Hugo warned. "Don't take advantage just because she's in a mood."

"She's not in a mood, you're in a mood," Alexia argued. "And I'm not taking advantage."

She skipped happily out of the room, seemingly unaware that she was the only person in the house not utterly miserable.

"She's taking advantage," Hugo muttered.

"She's getting a taste for the high life," Holly replied. "Pizza yesterday, popcorn today."

"There will be a sugar ban by the end of the week," he said solemnly.

"Probably," Holly agreed. She pulled her leg up and tucked it underneath her. She looked at him. "What's up?"

"Nothing," he mumbled.

"Sure. You just look like someone cancelled your birthday for no reason."

"It's stupid." He focused his attention on his phone, but she could tell he wasn't looking at anything specific.

"It's a girl," she surmised. "Or a guy?"

"Girl," he corrected. "But it's stupid."

"I bet it isn't." She reached forward and snagged a satsuma from the coffee table fruit bowl. "There's a reason why the vast majority of TV is about relationships, because they cause the most trouble in the world. That and war. You're not starting a war, are you?"

He smirked. "No."

"Good, I think your mother would have something to say."

"Don't tell her anything, I don't want to bother her," Hugo said.

"I don't think she'd consider anything that's upsetting you as a bother to her. But, I promise that anything you tell me will stay between us," she said.

Hugo sighed and lowered his phone to his lap.

"There's this girl, Kristine. Her best friend Penny told me that she's interested in me—"

"Kristine or Penny?" Holly asked.

"Penny told me that Kristine is interested in me," he amended. "So, I wrote her a note, but Jimmy Spicer got hold of it and read it out in class. Now everyone thinks I'm an idiot and Kristine won't even look at me."

Feeling like an idiot and being ignored by the object of your desire were both phenomena Holly could relate to.

"That must have been horribly embarrassing," she agreed. She jabbed her thumb into the clementine and started to peel it.

He looked at her. "Well?"

"Well what?"

"Aren't you going to give me some advice?" he asked.

"I dunno, am I?" She picked out a segment. "Do you *want* some advice? Or some satsuma?"

He held out his hand, and she placed a segment in his palm.

"That's normally what people do, give advice, try to fix things," Hugo said.

"Do you want me to try?" she asked.

He slowly nodded.

She considered the situation for a moment. "See, the biggest problem you have is giving a shit what other people think. And if you tell your mom I just said a curse word I'll tell her I caught you drinking whisky or something, so don't even go there."

He smiled at her and chewed on the piece of satsuma.

"Do you like this Kristine?"

"Yeah," he admitted. "She's really pretty and smart."

"Okay, then you need to cut through all the noise and focus on what you want. Humans, especially teenagers, get bored easily. If nothing is happening in their life, then they will tear down other people. The key is to ignore it and focus on what you want. It's really hard, especially at school. But you need to think, in ten years do you want to have not embarrassed yourself in front of James Spicer, or do you want to have dated Kristine? Because, sad fact of life, Hugo, James Spicer will be a bully no matter what. If it wasn't that note, it would have been your hair, your shoes, your accent. Something."

"But everyone heard the note, everyone knows," Hugo complained.

Holly shrugged. "So? You like a popular, attractive, clever girl. What's so terrible about that? You have good taste and you took a chance on getting what you wanted. Okay, now Kristine is probably embarrassed because all the attention is on her and how she'll react. If she says no, then they'll say something, if she says yes, then they'll say something else. She can't win either."

"So it's hopeless," Hugo said.

"As long as you care about what other people think, yeah, it is pretty hopeless." She ate a piece of her fruit.

"You're not good at pep talks," he told her with a chuckle.

"Hey, I'm recovering from a brain injury. I'm not here to make you feel better." She winked to let him know she was joking.

He sighed and rested his head against the soft material of the sofa. "I get what you're saying, I shouldn't worry so much about what other people think. But those other people are ruining my chances with Kristine."

"No," Holly argued, "you're ruining your chances. Let me guess, you stormed out of class, moped about all day, avoided her as she avoided you… right?"

"Pretty much."

"Do you have her number? Are you connected on social media somehow?" Holly asked.

Hugo started to look panicked. "Well… yeah."

"Well, it's time to rip the Band-Aid off. The longer you leave it, the worse it will get. Contact her now, get it sorted out."

He sat up, colour rising on his cheeks and the start of a sweat forming on his brow.

"It's your choice," she said. "But, you could end this week with a date with Kristine if you wanted to. Or at least a good chance of it. Girls mature faster than boys, and you're mature for your age. Those other boys are showing how immature they are. You could swoop in and show Kristine how much better you are."

Hugo looked nervously at his phone. "You... you think?"

"Sure!" Holly sat up. "I'll help you if you like. What are we thinking? Email? Twitter? How many characters have we got to work with?"

Hugo grabbed his phone and shuffled closer to Holly. "You think this will work?"

"I don't know, buddy. But if we don't try, then you'll be miserable for a long time. At least this way we can get it sorted out and then you can move on."

"That's true," he agreed.

He unlocked his phone and they huddled in the corner of the sofa, composing a message to send. Alexia returned with a mountain of popcorn that she seemed to have no intention of sharing. She took one look at Hugo's phone and shook her head. She turned the movie back on and scoffed into her popcorn.

Victoria looked up at the knock on the study door. She dreaded whoever it was on the other side. She wasn't prepared for a second round with Hugo. Holly was acting bizarrely, and Alexia seemed to have become a bottomless pit of sweet treats.

"Come," she called.

The door opened, and Hugo stood there.

Her heart sank. She wasn't strong enough to argue with him again.

"Hey, can I come in?" he asked.

"Of course." She closed her laptop lid.

He closed the study door behind him and sat on the sofa. He fidgeted nervously with his hands, and she was reminded of when he did the same thing as a young boy awaiting a reprimand for being naughty. Not that Hugo was often naughty. That was why his outburst had bothered her. She didn't know if she could cope with her oldest child completely reversing his personality as he became a teenager.

"I wanted to apologise," he said.

She blinked in surprise.

"I didn't mean what I said when you got home. I was in a really bad mood, and then I said some things I shouldn't have and I'm sorry."

"Oh." To say his apology was unexpected was an incredible understatement.

"I just felt stupid," he continued, "this thing happened at school. About a girl. It just sounded so childish and stupid. But I shouldn't have taken it out on you."

"It's okay, I understand." She didn't understand, not entirely. But she was getting an apology and so forgiveness and understanding were expected of her.

"I won't do it again," he promised. He looked down at his hands, clearly worried that it was a promise he wouldn't be able to keep.

"It's fine. As long as you talk to me," she said. "So, there's a girl?" she fished.

"There is now." A smile spread across his face. "We're seeing each other for lunch on Saturday."

Victoria shifted a little uncomfortably. Her little boy

had rudely turned into a grown man without her permission. And had a date.

"It's Kristine Andersen, you know her parents," Hugo added, seeing his mother's growing panic.

She frowned as she tried to recall the name. "Andersen? Oh, George?"

He nodded.

"You said there was a problem at school?" she asked.

"Yeah." He ran a hand through his thick hair and let out a sigh. "I wrote a note for her and the wrong people got hold of it and read it out. It was really embarrassing. That was why I was upset."

"That sounds terrible, sweetheart. Do I need to call the school?"

"No, it's fine. I spoke to Holly about it. She gave me some good advice."

Victoria swallowed nervously. Holly was giving her son dating advice. Wasn't that her role? What had Holly said?

"Don't worry, Mom." He chuckled. "She gave me good advice. She told me not to worry about the bullies and to rise above them. She told me to use my maturity to speak to Kristine, and we've been talking all evening."

"Good, good." She couldn't wipe the frown from her brow.

"Holly's great," Hugo said. "I'm glad she's here with us."

"I am, too," she confessed. No matter how muddied the situation became, she was still flying high on the relief that Holly was with her and safe. The girl's colour had returned to her cheeks, there was a bounce in her step, and it even looked like a couple of pounds were returning to her gaunt frame.

"Don't… you know, don't mess it up," Hugo said softly.

She chuckled. "Oh, it doesn't matter at this point."

"What do you mean?"

"It doesn't matter what I do or say now. I believe Holly's memories will return and that will seal my fate. Once she remembers how I treated her as my assistant, she won't be able to get away from me quickly enough." It felt good to finally say the words, to voice her fears. She was protecting herself by staying away. If she didn't get attached to Holly, she wouldn't feel the devastating blow when Holly walked away. For a second time. "She probably already remembers if her behaviour is anything to go by."

"Then you need to get there first," he said. He sat forward on the sofa and looked like he meant business. "Tell her."

She shook her head. "No, I-I can't do that. It's ridiculous."

"It isn't," he insisted. "You need to be brave and tell her what you're worried about. You like her, you must for her to be here. And let's face it, you could do with a real friend like Holly."

"Of course I like her. And, yes, she's a wonderful person and would make a fine friend. But I can't say anything. She can't guarantee how she'll react when her memories return. Even with the best intentions, once the floodgates open…" She shook he head. "It's ludicrous to think that we could be friends. The past doesn't forget, Hugo."

"Maybe not forget, but forgive. You weren't that bad to her, were you?"

She shrugged her shoulders. "I was… me."

"Pretty bad then," Hugo joked.

She glared at him, and he laughed lightly.

"I still think you should say something. You can't hide in here forever," he said.

"I'm not hiding, I'm working." She crossed her arms.

"Yeah, you're coming home earlier than usual to work from home? Doesn't make any sense. Do you want to know what I think?"

"Not particularly," she said.

"I think you want to join in and get involved, but you're afraid. So you come home but then you worry about Holly remembering and getting mad and leaving. You could fix that by just talking to her, Mom."

"Maybe. But it's not happening. Holly is here to rest and recover, not to have more stress piled onto her by me." She lifted her laptop lid to get back to work. "And you're not to say anything to her either. I'm deadly serious, Hugo."

She pinned him with a stern stare. He slowly nodded and held up his hands. "It's not my place to say anything anyway," he pointed out.

"It isn't," she agreed.

"But think about it," he added. He stood up. "I'm going to bed."

She looked at her watch and was shocked to see how many hours had passed.

He walked around the desk and placed a soft kiss in her hair. "Night, Mom."

"Good night, sweetheart."

CHAPTER THIRTY-FOUR

Holly returned several books to the shelves in Victoria's study. Despite the endless doctors' appointments and meetings with various specialists to get her life back on track, her days dragged.

It had been two weeks since the children had returned home, almost three since she had started to live at the Hastings residence. The early morning and the evenings were wonderful. Alexia was a bundle of fun and energy, always dragging Holly around to do anything from watching movies to playing games. Hugo was intelligent and focused, like his mother. Holly adored spending time with him. They debated political matters and he spoke about what he was learning in school.

And then there was Victoria. Now and then she'd become involved in whatever the three of them were doing, but then she'd remember herself and pull back. Holly just couldn't understand it. One moment Victoria was laughing and joking while they played a video game, the next she was coming up with an excuse to close herself in her office.

Holly then spent the quiet days replaying conversations in her head and trying to understand what had caused Victoria to leave.

Alexia had broached the subject a couple of times. She told Holly not to give up on her mom, saying that Victoria clearly had feelings for her but was struggling to show them. Holly couldn't see whatever Alexia was seeing. She was wondering if the girl was merely projecting her wishes for a cohesive family unit onto Holly and Victoria.

She couldn't blame Alexia, she imagined it must be a lonely existence to be the only person in the house who was full of energy and bounce. Hugo and Victoria were serious and steady. Alexia just wanted to have fun.

As the days passed, Holly's hope grew cold. Where she had once felt certain that Victoria felt more for her than simple friendship, now she doubted herself. Just because Victoria was being kind and generous, it didn't mean anything.

And Victoria's refusal to spend too much time with them convinced Holly that she was deluded to think someone like Victoria would want anything to do with her.

She sighed as she slid the last book into place.

It was time to leave. As luxurious, comfortable, and homely as it was living with the Hastings family, it had to end.

She'd quickly started to feel like one of the family, and that was dangerous. She was nothing more than a former assistant who had an accident and snagged on the heartstrings of a wealthy woman. Guilt was all Victoria felt. Guilt that would be alleviated if Holly left.

Not to mention the fact that she needed to get out now,

before she became more integrated into the family. It would already be a huge pull for her to leave. Every extra day she spent there would just make leaving worse.

She already spent her long and quiet days wondering if Hugo was acing the math test he was so confident of, or if Alexia had managed to get through an entire lesson without her grouchy science teacher telling her off for chatting. And if Victoria was looking after herself at work and remembering to eat.

Of course, she had to leave. And soon.

She had enough money in her savings account to put a deposit into a small room in a house share in Weehawken, across the river. And she had a couple of part-time temping job offers lined up that would fit around her doctors' appointments, which had been reduced to a few days a week. It was a giant leap into the unknown. But she couldn't stay.

The thing that devastated her the most was the finality of it all. When she left, she would be leaving permanently. She was a nobody. She had no reason to come and watch a movie with the children. No reason to call up Victoria and ask her if she finally decided to go with the greyscale background for the summer suit selection.

When she said goodbye and stepped out of the door, it would be forever. People like her didn't cross paths with people like the Hastings.

She walked across the room and ran her fingers along Victoria's desk. She'd tell them that evening. Her heart broke when she considered what Alexia's reaction would be. Hopefully Victoria would allow them to stay in touch by email.

She took a deep breath, taking in Victoria's scent that lingered in the air.

This room she'd miss the most. Even though it was the place where Victoria hid the most, she'd still managed to spend time with the older woman in this room. She'd attempted to assist her, like the old days. She'd read books from the extensive collection. She'd even caught Victoria asleep in the armchair one evening.

She smiled to herself. She'd have the memories, somewhat ironically.

She walked towards the hallway, turning off the light and closing the door.

CHAPTER THIRTY-FIVE

Victoria put her handbag on the hallway table and started to remove her coat. It had been a long day, one where getting away early was simply impossible. She'd phoned earlier and asked Holly if she would mind watching the children. Holly, as predicted, had said it wasn't a problem and to get home when she could.

She hung her coat in the closet and frowned as she heard footsteps hammering down the stairs. She turned around.

"Mom!" Alexia cried out, tears streaming down her face.

"Darling?" Victoria started to panic. She walked towards her daughter, her arms outstretched.

Alexia threw herself into Victoria's arms.

"Darling, what is it?" Victoria held her tightly, a thousand thoughts running through her mind at what had Alexia in such a state.

"Mom, you have to fix it. You have to," Alexia mumbled.

Victoria knew in that second that she would fix it.

Whatever it was. Whatever had reduced her darling girl to tears would be fixed.

"Fix what? You're frightening me, sweetheart."

Alexia took a step back and rubbed at her red face. "Holly's leaving. She's got a job, and she's going to leave in a couple of days."

Victoria felt her blood run cold at the news. She'd been expecting it, but, as long as she hid herself away in her office, she could pretend that everything was fine. Of all the things that Alexia could demand she fix, this was the one that she knew would be impossible.

"It's your fault, you have to fix it," Alexia said, her face becoming impossibly redder.

"I-I can't fix it, sweetheart. There's nothing I can do, Holly has her own life, and if she chooses to go and—"

Alexia wrenched herself out of her mother's grip. She looked up at her with a glare that was apparently genetic.

Victoria froze. Alexia's face was venomous at not hearing what she wanted to hear.

"I hate you," Alexia said. She burst into tears and run back up the stairs.

Victoria stood in shock. She knew she should do something, but she had no idea what. Holly was leaving. Alexia blamed her, correctly so.

She couldn't fix it. Too many things had happened in the past to be fixed like that. Not that she could adequately explain such things to Alexia.

She brought her hands up to rub her upper arms. She wasn't used to not knowing what to do and she didn't like the sensation.

"She doesn't mean it."

She turned around to see Hugo appear from the kitchen. He bit into an apple and leaned on the doorframe.

"She sounded like she meant it," Victoria said.

She could feel tears forming and quickly turned away. Hugo didn't need to see her weakness.

She felt an arm around her shoulder.

"Come on," he said softly, "let's go into the study."

He guided her across the hallway and into her sanctuary. When they were safely inside, he closed the door behind them and walked her over to the armchair.

The touching gesture caused a few tears to fall. She plucked a tissue from the box that sat on the side table and dabbed at her eyes.

Hugo grabbed a bottle of water from the mini-fridge in the corner of the room and poured a glass for his mother.

"Thank you," she said through a sniffle. She took the glass and sipped the cool water.

"You really like her, don't you?" Hugo asked.

"Alexia? Of course I do! She's my daught—"

"I don't mean Alexia, Mom. She's said mean things to you before and it didn't affect you like this. I mean Holly. You… it's… more than just friendship, isn't it?"

"No," Victoria denied. "I don't know what you're insinuating, but Holly is just an ex-employee. Nothing more."

She dabbed at the remaining tears and sat up a little taller.

"I'm just upset with Alexia's reaction, and it was a long day," she added.

"Mom, I've seen how you look at her. How she looks at you. I know something's going on. And I know you've dated women…"

She nearly dropped the glass of water. "Wh—How?"

"The Internet. Before Dad, you were seen out with women. Please only deny it if it's not true," he said softly. "Don't deny it because of what you worry I'll think of you. Nearly everyone at school says they're bisexual because they want to be cool. It's not like it's a thing anymore. If you're bi, you're bi. Or gay. Or whatever other label you want."

She lifted the glass to her lips and downed a couple of large mouthfuls of water to quench her suddenly dry throat.

So the Internet had outed her. She wondered why she hadn't heard about it before. Then again, there were hundreds of thousands of news outlets and blogs, so maybe it wasn't a surprise that some sailed under her radar.

There was no need to lie about it now. Hugo was mature enough to understand that his mother had a life outside of being a parent.

"I've never really put a label on it," she admitted. "After I married your father I thought that was that. That it was all rather irrelevant. And then, after the divorce, I didn't think I'd have to think about it. Who wants to date the dragon lady?"

"Anyone would be lucky to have you," he said sincerely.

She put her glass on the table and walked over to where he leaned on her desk. She pulled him into a big hug.

"Anyone would be lucky to have you as their son," she told him.

He wrapped his arms around her and held her tightly, reminding her just how big he was growing and that he wasn't her little boy anymore.

"I don't believe you, by the way," he said, his chin perched on her head.

"About what?" she asked.

"That you were just upset by Alexia's reaction."

"Yes, well, that's your prerogative, I suppose."

"It's not too late," he said.

She stepped back and cupped his cheek with her hand. "It is, darling. It is. Whether or not I have feelings for Holly is utterly irrelevant. She's young, I'm old, divorced, I have two awful children who are practically monsters."

He chuckled. "Hey, *I* didn't say I hated you."

"No, thank goodness." She took a step back and grabbed another tissue. She felt she looked a mess, so she wanted to repair any damage before she set about dealing with Alexia.

"Holly didn't mean to tell us," he added. "I think she wanted to talk to you first. But then Alexia was trying to get her to take us to the movies next week and Holly had to come clean and tell us. She's downstairs, she felt bad for upsetting Alexia, and I suggested she give her some space."

Victoria swallowed. She examined her reflection in the mirror above the sofa.

"She has a job?"

"Yes, receptionist, part-time. It fits around her medical appointments," he said.

"I see. And... somewhere to live? Please tell me she's not still thinking about a hostel."

"She mentioned sharing a house, renting a room. It's, like, a million miles away, though." He wrinkled his nose. "You have to take New Jersey Transit to get there."

"I see."

"So, she's ruining her life," Hugo added. "Taking the

first job she can find, it's not what she wants. She said it will pay the bills, but she won't be happy."

"She has her own life, Hugo, I can't stop her."

"You can talk to her. She looks up to you."

Victoria laughed. "No, she doesn't."

"She does. She talks about you like you're her hero. While you're down here, hiding from us and pretending to be so busy with work. She's watching movies, playing games, helping us with homework, and all the time she's telling us how great you are and how lucky we are to have you."

She swallowed again. She turned around and took a deep breath.

"That may be. But first I need to check on your sister."

Hugo shrugged. "Whatever," he mumbled. Clearly, he'd had enough bashing his head against the brick wall that was his mother's stubbornness. Thank goodness.

She couldn't think of anything to say to him. So, she walked silently out of the study. Her mind was spinning with new information. This wasn't how she had expected the evening to go, but she supposed things had been building. Something had to give eventually.

The games room was quiet, the living room, too. It seemed that Alexia had gone straight to her room to sulk. Victoria walked up another flight of stairs to the top floor of the house. She approached Alexia's door and gently knocked.

"Sweetheart? Can I come in?"

She waited a few moments.

Silence.

"Alexia?"

She realised the door wasn't quite closed and softly pushed on the door. It opened to reveal a darkened room. She stepped in and squinted while her eyes adjusted to the lack of light.

"Alexia?" she asked.

She turned on the light and saw that the room was empty.

"Damn," she mumbled to herself. If Alexia wasn't in her room or the main living areas, she must be in Holly's room. Presumably throwing herself on the floor and begging the girl to stay.

While she didn't feel strong enough to confront Holly just yet, she knew she had to speak with Alexia. With a deep breath, she started to make her way downstairs.

CHAPTER THIRTY-SIX

Holly heard the footsteps coming down the stairs and paused her writing. She had no idea how Victoria would react to the news of her leaving, or to the fact that she had told the children before her. She suspected not well. Especially after she heard Alexia's outburst twenty minutes ago.

Victoria appeared in the doorway. Holly offered her a tight smile.

"I'm sorry to interrupt," Victoria said. She fidgeted with her hands as she tried to clasp them in front of herself.

"You're not interrupting," Holly told her. "I'm the one who should be apologising. I didn't mean to upset Alexia. I didn't want to tell her until after I had spoken with you, but she kind of cornered me and then wheedled it out of me."

"She has a talent for wheedling information," Victoria noted.

Victoria's eyes drifted to the newly purchased secondhand suitcase that sat on the bench at the end of the bed. She opened her mouth to speak and then snapped it closed again.

"May I speak with her?" Victoria asked.

Holly frowned. "With?"

"My daughter," Victoria pressed. "She's not upstairs, so I assume she's here… somewhere?"

"She's not here, I haven't seen her since I told her I was leaving."

Victoria's body tensed, and she took a step back out into the hallway. She looked towards the kitchenette.

"Are you sure?"

Holly closed her journal and stood up. Something didn't feel right about this.

"Definitely," she replied, "she must be upstairs."

Victoria was already returning up the stairs, this time with Holly right behind her. On the next floor, Victoria started to search the rooms. Holly went up another flight and searched the living room and the games room.

Hugo's bedroom door was wide open, and she leaned her head in to see if Alexia was there. She could hear the music blasting through his headphones. He looked at her inquisitively, and she shook her head, not wanting to worry him yet.

In the hallway she met a panicked Victoria.

"Anything?"

Holly shook her head. Together they scrambled up the final flight of stairs, Holly taking them two at a time. She went straight to Alexia's room and looked inside, checking under the bed and behind the curtain just to be sure.

She heard Victoria checking the other rooms. Her voice was calling out for her daughter, increasing in volume each time.

Holly checked Alexia's desk and noticed her phone and the small handbag she used were both gone.

Victoria burst into the room.

"Have you seen her?" she demanded. She breezed past Holly and started to check the bed and the curtains in the same way Holly had done moments before.

"No, and her phone is gone." Holly had already pulled her own phone out of her jeans pocket and was starting to dial Alexia's number.

Victoria let out a gasp. She dropped onto the edge of Alexia's bed. She picked up one of the fluffy pink pillows and held it tightly on her lap. The colour started to drain from her face. Her eyes stared into nothingness.

The phone went straight through to voicemail.

"It's Holly, you're not in trouble, but you have to call us back immediately. We're very worried, okay? Just, please, call us back."

Holly fired off a quick text to Hugo and asked him to come upstairs. She could see that Victoria was rapidly starting to fall apart. She knelt in front of her.

"She's going to be fine, we'll find her," Holly promised.

Victoria looked towards her, but her eyes were vacant. Holly couldn't imagine the terror she was experiencing. Knowing that her eight-year-old daughter was roaming the streets of New York alone.

Hugo walked in. "What's happening?" He looked at his mother in concern.

"Do you know where your sister is?" Holly asked as Victoria remained silent.

"No, I didn't see her again after she shouted at Mom…"

Hugo looked around the room. The penny dropped, and he realised why his mother was in pieces. "I'll check the house again."

He turned and left the room.

"Check everything," Holly shouted after him. "Twice."

"Got it!" he shouted back.

Holly went to Alexia's desk and lifted the lid on her MacBook.

"Victoria, what's the password?"

She turned around to see Victoria was still staring blankly into nothingness.

"Victoria!" she snapped. "Password."

Victoria blinked a few times. "Oh, yes, um. I…" She looked shocked, the information not coming to her in the heat of the moment.

Holly walked over and kneeled in front of her again. She took her hands.

"She'll be fine, she's probably gone to a friend's house or something. Her computer might have a clue. Just take a deep breath with me, okay? Let's breathe in." She took a deep breath and gestured for Victoria to do the same.

Remarkably, she did.

"And out."

Victoria repeated the motion.

"It's Izzy789," Victoria said.

Holly went back to the computer and unlocked it. There were no windows open. She accessed the browser history, but Alexia hadn't been on the computer all evening. Victoria stood behind her, looking at the screen and sighing at its lack of information.

"Has she ever done this before?" Holly asked.

"No, never."

"Would she contact her dad?"

Victoria laughed bitterly. "No, she can't stand him."

"How much cash does she have here? Does she have access to any bank cards?"

Victoria stepped away and started to pace the room.

"She has a card for her bank account, but it's kept in my safe in the study, she can't open it. As for cash, she gets pocket money. And she has some emergency money. But I don't know how much that is." She paused and shook her head. "I have no idea how much cash she might have."

Holly stood up and took Victoria's hands in her own. "This isn't your fault, if anything… it's mine."

"The blame game again, really, Holly?" Victoria snapped. She pulled away and sat on the edge of Alexia's bed.

Holly ran her hands through her hair. She knew Victoria was referring to her accident, obviously she still felt that she shouldered the blame for that. It was infuriating that Victoria felt she was to blame when Holly knew it was her own fault. She had walked away. Did Victoria really feel that she had that much control over her?

Back at her sides, her fists tightened, fingernails digging into her palms. Then she remembered the serious situation and took a cleansing breath.

Hugo ran into the room, out of breath and with his shoes in his hand.

"She's not here, her jacket is gone, and so are her favourite shoes. I'm going to go look for her."

Victoria jumped to her feet. "No, you're not leaving,"

she said firmly, though her voice quivered. She started to rub her upper arms.

"Yes, I am," Hugo argued. "The longer we leave it, the more chance—"

"I'll go with him," Holly interrupted whatever he was about to say. She agreed with him that searching for Alexia was the right thing to do, but she also understood Victoria's reticence to let him out of her sight.

"But—" Victoria started.

"We'll be fine, it's for the best," Holly said. "You stay here in case she comes home."

"Should we call the police?" Hugo asked. He leaned against the doorframe and slipped on his shoes.

"She hasn't been missing long enough," Holly pointed out.

"They'll make an exception for Mom," he said.

"I'll call," Victoria agreed, her voice so soft that Holly struggled to hear despite standing beside her.

"Okay, let's go," Hugo said.

He turned to leave, but Victoria snapped out of her trance and grabbed his arm before he did. She enveloped him in a hug, grasping at his shoulders to hold him as tightly as possible.

"Be careful," she told him.

Holly looked on awkwardly. She wanted to comfort Victoria and tell her that everything was going to be okay, but she knew that Victoria wasn't likely to believe her nor appreciate the gesture.

Hugo pulled away and gave his mother a serious look before turning and leaving the room.

"We'll be in touch," Holly promised.

Victoria nodded but remained silent.

Holly raced down the stairs in pursuit of Hugo. She was already thinking of all the places Alexia might go, trying to think like her and predict her movements. She just hoped, shooting a quick look to the heavens, that nothing had happened.

CHAPTER THIRTY-SEVEN

Victoria sat on the stairs. Her gaze flicked between the front door and the phone she clutched in her hands. It had been an hour since Holly and Hugo had left, and there had been no word.

Her chest felt tight, and her breathing was shallow. She could only imagine the state she must look, feeble and broken.

She couldn't help the bitter laugh that escaped her and rattled around the empty hallway. *How the mighty have fallen,* she thought. *Just a few hours ago I was on top of the world, running my empire. Now I have lost my youngest child.*

She stared at her phone again, fearful that she would somehow miss an important call or message. She'd called the police and informed them of the situation. While an official report couldn't be created, she had the commissioner's reassurance that word would be circulated to relevant officers on patrol in their neighbourhood.

The realisation that she had no idea where Alexia would go or what she would do was terrifying. Did she really know so little about her only daughter? Alexia had complained that her mother worked too hard. She'd often referred to *Arrival* as her older sister, and occasionally, Victoria's favourite child.

Of course, Victoria had done everything she could to quash that. But now she wondered if maybe there was a grain of truth in it. Did she rank work over family? If only for the reason that work would kick, scream, and fall apart if she were absent, whereas family would do their best to forgive her.

If Alexia came home, things would change. They would have to.

Every award and accolade meant nothing if she would ever have to experience another second of this sheer terror.

The doorbell rang.

She nearly tripped over herself in her hurry to get to the door. The lock stuck for a moment, but she eventually yanked the door open. Two police officers stood on the doorstep, Alexia in between them.

She looked furious but healthy.

"Miss Hastings," the female officer greeted. "We found your daughter in the park."

Victoria felt her eyebrows raise. The very idea of Alexia alone in Central Park at night made her legs wobble.

Alexia rushed past her and into the house, not giving her mother a second glance.

Victoria watched her climb the stairs before dragging her eyes back to the officers.

"Thank you so much."

"We're just doing our job. Have a good evening, ma'am."

Before she had a chance to form a sentence, they were on their way again. She closed the front door and leaned on it as she took a deep, shaky breath.

She fired off a quick text message to Hugo and Holly to let them know that Alexia was safely home.

"Alexia?" she called as she climbed the stairs.

"Go away," the muffled response indicated that Alexia was in her room.

Victoria made quick work of the stairs and stood outside the closed bedroom door. She wanted to shove the door to one side and hold Alexia tightly, but she knew her presence wasn't welcome yet.

She knocked on the door. "Darling? Please can we talk?"

"No." She sounded like she was crying.

Victoria wasn't about to stand by and listen to the sound of tears.

"I'm coming in," she announced. She grabbed the door handle and entered the room.

Alexia was curled up on her bed, her back to the room. She hugged her favourite teddy bear to her chest.

A sudden shiver ran down Victoria's spine at what might have happened. She wondered if she'd ever get over the panic.

She sat on the edge of the bed and placed her hand on Alexia's hip.

"I don't want Holly to go," Alexia mumbled.

"I don't either," Victoria confessed.

"Then tell her she has to stay, she'll listen to you."

"She won't, darling. She has to live her own life, and I'm not her boss anymore."

Alexia turned over. Her eyes were red and her cheeks puffy.

"I don't want her to go," she repeated. "I hate it without her. I'm so l-lonely. I hate being here."

Victoria heard a gasp escape her mouth. She had no idea that Alexia was so unhappy at home. There was a possibility that Alexia was being dramatic, but for some reason she didn't think that was the case. If Alexia had wanted to pull on her mother's heartstrings in the past, then this would surely have been brought up. But this was the first she was hearing of it, and that made it more real.

She knew that Holly spent a lot of time with her daughter and had seen that Alexia enjoyed that. But the possibility that Alexia was lonely had never even occurred to her. It made sense. Alexia's brother rarely spent time with her, Victoria was rarely home and certainly unable to spend time with her when she was.

She kicked off her shoes and lay down beside her daughter, pulling her into a hug.

"I'm so sorry, darling. I didn't know. We'll… we'll change things. It will be better, I promise."

Alexia wrapped her arms around her and burrowed her face into her chest.

"But I want Holly here. You have to work and Hugo doesn't want to play with me."

"I'll work less," Victoria promised. She was already mentally moving her schedule around. Work was important but nearly losing her daughter had quickly reversed her priorities. "You must never run away again. Ever. I was so scared, anything could have happened to you."

"I'm sorry; I didn't think and then I didn't know what to do because I thought you'd be mad."

"Oh, darling, I'm only mad at myself."

Alexia sniffled and sat up. She fixed Victoria with a determined look.

"Are you *sure* we can't make Holly stay?"

Victoria sat up, too. She took Alexia's hands in hers.

"I'm sorry, no. We have to let Holly live her life. If she wants to leave, then she must be allowed to leave."

"But she doesn't want to leave, she's just sad."

Victoria dried Alexia's tearstained cheeks with her thumbs.

"What makes you say that, darling?"

"She just is. She told me she can't stay here forever because she's not one of us. I told her that she was, but she didn't believe me. She said she had to go. I don't understand."

Victoria didn't truly understand either. The comment made no sense. She'd assumed that Holly's journals, and maybe some recollected memories, had nudged her to realise that she was living under the same roof as the devil. Under those circumstances, she couldn't blame the girl for wanting to leave.

"Where is Holly?" Alexia sniffled.

"Out looking for you, with Hugo. We were all very worried."

Alexia blushed. "I'm sorry."

"Just promise me you won't do it again," Victoria said. "If you're upset then come to me or go to your room, but never leave the house like that again."

"I promise." Alexia kneeled on the bed and leaned in for another big hug.

Victoria ignored the awkward position and held her daughter as tight as she could. She still hadn't recovered from the shock of almost losing this little girl.

She heard the front door slamming closed and voices calling out, but neither mother nor daughter wanted to let go of each other and call back.

It was only a few moments before Victoria could hear Holly and Hugo rushing up the stairs.

Holly was first into the room and threw her arms around both Alexia and Victoria.

"Are you okay?" Holly asked frantically.

"I'm okay, I'm sorry," Alexia replied.

"No need to be sorry, just be safe," Holly instructed.

She pulled away from the hug and looked at Victoria seriously. "Are you okay?"

Victoria hadn't expected to be asked and slowly nodded her head.

"Don't do that again, brat," Hugo said. The relief was clear on his face despite his disinterested tone.

"I won't," Alexia replied, smiling at her brother's small display of worry.

Victoria watched him leave the bedroom and then realised that Holly's eyes were still on her, still concerned.

"I'm fine," she promised softly.

"Holly, do you really have to go?" Alexia said.

"Alexia," Victoria warned.

"It's okay," Holly said. "I do, I'm sorry, but I do."

"Can you visit me?" Alexia begged in her best whining tone.

"Um." Holly looked blankly at Victoria.

"Of course you can," Victoria replied. She'd invited Holly into her home and was surprised the girl thought she would be banished so easily. "We'd welcome it. In fact, we'd be very angry if you didn't come and visit. All of us."

Holly looked at her curiously before a smile spread across her face. She turned to face Alexia. "Looks like I'll be visiting you very soon, I wouldn't want your mom to be angry." She winked.

It was sometime later when Victoria had finally managed to put Alexia to bed. She was in her study nursing a glass of red wine. She'd already emailed the office to advise them that an emergency would see her arriving in the office late and leaving early. It was unprecedented, but it would be the first of many changes.

"Can I come in?"

She saw Holly standing by the door and nodded. The girl walked into the study and sat on the sofa.

"How's Alexia?" Holly asked.

"It took a while for her to get to sleep, but she seems to be okay. I don't think I'll be sleeping tonight."

"Me neither. That was scary stuff," Holly admitted. "I'm sorry. I know it was my fault."

"On the contrary, it was mine," Victoria said. "While she was upset that you were leaving, it just went to highlight that she was devastated at the thought of things going back to the way they were before you arrived. She said she felt lonely before."

Victoria walked over to the desk where the half empty bottle of red sat. She poured herself another glass and gestured with it towards Holly. Holly shook her head.

"I can't blame her," Victoria continued. "I'm rarely home, and when I am, I'm consumed with work. Hugo tries to entertain her, but he's a teenage boy with his own life to live. I just hadn't realised how hard it has been for Alexia. I should be thanking you for highlighting the issue."

"I'm still sorry. I triggered her reaction, she ran out of the house and anything could have happened." Holly worried her lip.

Victoria sipped some wine. She stared at the bookcase and considered it was time to reorganise her collection. Anything to take her mind off the subject of what might have happened to Alexia if the police hadn't managed to find her.

"So," Victoria said, "you're leaving us?"

Holly sat up a little straighter. "Yes. I can't thank you enough for everything you've done for me, but I need to start fending for myself. I have some money in my savings account and I am able to work, so it makes sense for me to start to rebuild my life."

"I see. And when will this be happening? Where will you go?"

"Tomorrow," Holly said.

Victoria felt her pulse start to race. *So soon?*

"I've found a house in Weehawken with a room for rent. There's six of us, so I won't get lonely. I've met them and they all seem really nice. All girls. Well, one guy, but he's engaged to the girl who placed the ad online. He is hardly—"

"And a job?" Victoria asked to cut off the rambling.

"A part-time receptionist job, next door to the clinic where I'm having my physiotherapy. So that works out really well."

"Hm." Victoria turned to look at the framed copies of *Arrival* that lined the wall behind her desk. They were the issues that had broken sales records, the ones where she had pushed boundaries and been rewarded handsomely. Suddenly they didn't mean so much to her.

"Are you sure you won't consider… staying?" Victoria asked, refusing to make eye contact as she did.

"I… think it's best if I go," Holly said.

She remembers, Victoria thought. *Or she's read enough of those damned journals to know everything that I ever said to her.*

"I see," she said. "The children will miss you, and I meant what I said; please come and visit us."

"I will," Holly promised.

"And soon," Victoria added for good measure. She kept her back to Holly, unwilling to turn around and meet her eyes.

"I will, once I've settled in. I don't have much stuff, so it won't be long." Holly chuckled softly.

Victoria remained silent. She stared at the framed issues.

"I should go to bed. I hope you manage to get some sleep," Holly said, clearly unable to stay in the stifling atmosphere any longer.

"Good night," Victoria offered, without turning.

She heard Holly leave the room and let out a deep sigh.

Holly was leaving. Sure, she'd visit once or twice to ensure that Alexia was well. But that would soon fade to nothing. After all this, Holly would vanish from her life once again. This time for good.

Victoria swigged some more wine.

It was inevitable, really. How could they ever have a friendship after all that had happened between them?

Maybe this was one of those times where the lesson would be learnt, but too late to make a difference.

She looked at the books that lined her shelves. Tonight would bring no sleep, so she might as well curl up with some good company.

CHAPTER THIRTY-EIGHT

Holly sat at the desk of her new job and let out a long sigh. She didn't think she had ever been so bored. The clock on the opposite wall had a sweeping second hand that glided around the large face. The longer Holly stared at it, the slower she felt it went.

She wondered how much job security there was as a receptionist for a company that never received any phone calls. It had been a week, and she'd put through eleven phone calls in total. But her boss seemed happy, giving her a thumbs up every time he walked through the reception area.

There was no computer, and so there was a lot of time to think.

The job wasn't awful, but it certainly wasn't fulfilling. It brought money in, and she could do it in her sleep. In fact, she was quite sure she had answered one call in her sleep. The office was warm and comfortable, which was more than could be said about the room in her new house share.

Everyone was very friendly, but the house was dilapidated to say the least. The first night she realised that there were some holes in the outer wall that had been covered with wallpaper. While that made it easier on the eyes, it certainly didn't help when the wind blew at night. It certainly didn't help her stop missing the tartan walls and cosy bedding of Victoria's guestroom.

She kept reminding herself that things would change soon. She'd soon have fewer appointments at the clinic, and the ones she had would be moved to evenings and weekends. That would leave her room for a proper full-time job. With that came money and the opportunity to move to a better home. Maybe a small apartment of her own.

The door to the outside world opened, and Gideon stepped into the reception area. He looked around and let out a sigh. "So, *this* is where hope went to die."

She laughed and rushed around the reception desk to hug him.

"I'm so glad to see you," she announced, throwing her arms around him.

He gathered her into the hug. "I'm glad to see you, too. Now, can we leave this place? I haven't had my shots updated."

She stood back and laughed again. "No, I have to wait for Janice to get here so I can hand over."

"Hand over what?" Gideon looked around the empty reception. He stage-whispered to Holly, "Nothing's happening."

She playfully slapped his arm. "Stop it, it's my job."

He rolled his eyes and flopped down on the sofa. "Fine, I'll starve while we wait for this Janice to come."

Holly returned to her seat. "Don't blame me, you're early."

He looked at his watch and raised an eyebrow. "I'm on Victoria Hastings time."

"Well, Victoria Hastings time doesn't operate here. We're on Eastern." She put her journal in her bag. "How is she?"

"Beastly," Gideon said with a little glee. "When I see her."

Holly hadn't spoken to Victoria or the children since she had left the previous week. She'd arranged to go to the house for dinner and was anxiously counting down the hours until Friday night.

"When you see her?" she questioned.

"She's spending more time at home. Working from home, and she's actually taken some vacation. You won't remember this, but vacation was a swear word back in the day. Things are changing at Casa Arrival."

Holly smiled to herself. So Victoria was keeping her promise to Alexia and spending more time at home.

"Have you spoken to her?" he asked, though she suspected he knew the answer.

"No," she said as she toyed idly with a file on her desk. "I've been super busy."

"Yes, I can see you're rushed off your feet."

She glared at him and he held up his hands in self-defence. "I jest, I jest."

The door opened, and Janice walked in with her heavy winter coat, giant bag with knitting needles sticking out the top, and various other tote bags. Janice liked to bring supplies for the long, quiet hours.

"Sorry I'm late, dear," she said. She turned to Gideon. "Hello, have you been seen to?"

"Not recently," Gideon replied.

"Ignore him," Holly called out. "For some reason, I'm having lunch with him, I must be crazy."

"Have another drink," Gideon pressed. He turned around and waved a waiter over.

"Nothing alcoholic," Holly said. She was already feeling quite tipsy after splitting a bottle of wine with him.

"Fine, fine, mocktails then," he said. "That way you at least *look* like you're having fun. Two Nojitos, please."

The waiter nodded and cleared away the empty plates before leaving again.

"You used to love Nojitos," Gideon told her. "Of course, mojitos were better. Then you'd tell me what was on your mind without the endless amount of wheedling I'm having to do."

"There's nothing on my mind," Holly insisted.

He looked at her sceptically. When she wouldn't relent, he put his elbow on the table and started counting points on his fingers. "You live in a room with more holes than actual wall. Your job is boring you to death. You can't stop asking about Victoria. You don't—"

"I've asked once about her," Holly interrupted. "Well, and then about the thing you said about the new marketing director. And about the luncheon. And… well, that award… wow, I have asked about her a lot, haven't I? I'm sorry, Gideon. I don't mean to go on and on about her."

Gideon smiled. "It's not like it's the first time."

Holly felt the blush rise on her cheeks. She knew she used to talk to Gideon a lot about her former boss. First to complain, then to admire. It was a habit she needed to break. While Victoria had invited her over for dinner, it was obviously to appease Alexia. The invites would soon fizzle out.

"I miss them," Holly admitted, the wine loosening her tongue.

"They miss you."

She laughed. "I'm sure Victoria is glad to be rid of me."

Gideon rolled his eyes. "God, you two are useless."

"What's *that* supposed to mean?" she demanded.

"Exactly what I said. The both of you. Utterly useless. I told you that Victoria always assumes the worst, remember?"

"Yes, I remember."

"What I didn't realise is that you're exactly the same."

She bristled at the insinuation. "I'm not. I mean… I-I don't do that." She knit her eyebrows and wondered if it was true or not. "I'm an optimist," she decided.

"Maybe, but not when it comes to Victoria. You are both automatically assuming the worst without talking to each other."

"What do you know?" she asked him. "Has she said something?"

Gideon shook his head. "I can't say. I can't betray a confidence."

The waiter placed two tall, clear glasses on the table, sprigs of mint and slices of lemon floating in them.

She wanted to pour the drink over his head. He knew

something, but he refused to share it. But his reluctance was also comforting, she knew she could trust him.

"So, what do I do?" she asked.

He shrugged his shoulders. "What do you want to do?"

"I don't know. I get the feeling that you're trying to lead me towards something, but I don't know what it is. I don't know what it is you want me to do." She picked up the drink and took a hearty swig. She smacked her lips, instantly remembering why it was one of her favourites.

Gideon stirred the straw in his drink and looked at her thoughtfully.

"Cards on the table," he said. "How do you feel about her?"

She slid down in her chair a little. "Gideon," she whinged.

"You can trust me, I won't tell a soul."

It wasn't telling him that worried her. It was admitting it to herself. She'd gotten as far as being able to confess that she thought Victoria was attractive and brilliant. There was more, she knew. But giving voice to it was a bad idea.

"In Paris, you told me you loved her," Gideon suddenly announced.

She gasped. "You… you never told me that! You told me that you suspected my feelings but I never said anything directly!"

"I did. I lied." He sipped at his drink.

"W-why?"

"Because you were living with Victoria at the time you asked me. Because you'd suffered some terrible accident and memory loss. I didn't know if I should tell you or not. I was sort of being honest. Prior to Paris you'd hinted at an…

admiration for her. But in Paris you told me that you were in love with her."

"Did… did I tell her?"

"I've no idea. It was the last real conversation we had before you left, went missing. At the time, I told you to ignore it, bury it."

She picked up her glass and, despite the lack of alcohol, took a few hefty gulps to brace herself. Not long before she left for Paris she'd journaled about dreams in which she was intimate with Victoria. Not to mention started drawing pictures of her. Clearly, her feelings were growing in intensity around that time.

"At that time," she mumbled. She looked up at him. "You said, *at that time* you told me to ignore it…"

He nodded slowly.

"But… now?" she asked hesitantly.

He licked his lips and leaned in closer, as if worried that Victoria's spies may be watching them at that very moment.

"Victoria isn't known for putting her feelings on display. To most people, she doesn't have any. But after you left, she changed. Assistants had left before, but this was different. And when she found you… she stayed behind in Paris to get you home. She put you up in her house. She… she acted about as un-Victoria as I have ever seen her."

Holly felt her hopes lift off the ground for a brief moment. Until reality hit and she remembered the decidedly cold shoulder that Victoria had given her when she was a guest in her home.

"I wondered the same, for a while," Holly confessed. "I kind of tried to flirt with her at her house, but… nothing. If anything, it had the opposite effect. She locked herself in her office to get away from me."

"Flirting?" he asked.

Holly rubbed the back of her neck. "Yeah, Alexia kind of called me out on having feelings for her mom."

Gideon covered his mouth to hold back a chuckle.

"So then I had to decide whether I would deny it, which Alexia wasn't going to buy. So, I decided to admit it and let her help me flirt. But it bombed, so badly. Victoria avoided me all the time, and it became harder and harder to be there."

"And that's why you left," he guessed.

"Yes. It was so nice being there, like this exquisite torture. Being close to her, being with a family. Neither really being mine and knowing it had to end one day. I made the decision to go before I got too attached. Or I tried to."

"I'm so sorry," he said. "It sounds like a hell of a situation."

"It was."

They sat in silence for a few moments, staring into their respective drink glasses, pretending to be interested in the floating mint sprigs.

"I wonder if your journal told you about the conversation we had at Gustav's? It was about three months before we left for Paris, when things were really coming to an end between you and Kate?" Gideon asked.

Holly searched her memory but couldn't think of the specific encounter he was alluding to.

"I'm not sure?"

"There was this guy." Gideon leaned back in his chair

and smiled at the memory. "Gorgeous. Well-dressed. I looked at him with interest, but then I thought about how young he probably was and I looked away. You asked me what I was thinking, and I told you. Do you know what you said?"

She shook her head.

"You asked me what I would remember more in six months, being rejected by him or having dated him."

She laughed. "Yes, that sounds like something I'd say."

"Well, I'd approached men before and been turned down. It wasn't the end of the world. Especially after some liquid courage. But for some reason at that moment, I got cold feet. You told me to go for it. You said that if he said no, then we'd drink all night and discuss how stupid his hair was anyway."

Holly smiled. "I wish I remembered that."

"Oh, I wish I could forget! He turned me down. I went over there, thinking I was on top of the world and he looked at me like I was his grandfather. Said no, politely, but still no. And then you and I drank all night and laughed at his stupid hair."

Holly bit back a giggle. "Oh, no! I'm so sorry!"

"Don't be. You reminded me to be brave. You reminded me that the fear of failure is so much worse than the actual event. So, I got turned down. We drank all night and had a blast. We were so hungover the next day and had to hide it from Victoria or she'd fire us both."

Holly felt her eyes bulge. She couldn't imagine Victoria not noticing that her second assistant and her second-in-command were hungover.

"And that's what I remember," Gideon was saying. "I

remember that you helped me find my courage, and then you propped me up when I fell."

Holly loved learning things that weren't in her journal. She wasn't surprised she didn't chronicle the evening, she probably couldn't even remember it the next day.

"Is this the part where you tell me to tell Victoria how I feel?" Holly asked.

Gideon shook his head. "No. That's for you to decide. Just remember to find your bravery. You once helped me when I lost mine, I want to make sure you haven't lost yours."

CHAPTER THIRTY-NINE

Holly arrived at the Hastings residence for dinner ten minutes early. She didn't want Victoria to perceive her as being late, primarily because Holly had decided that tonight would be the night. She had spent the last twenty-four hours planning how to corner Victoria and speak to her openly and honestly.

For once, the boring hours she spent at her dull reception job were put to good use. She dreamed up conversation openers, how to prevent Victoria's silences, and just how much she was willing to tell the woman.

The lunch with Gideon had opened her eyes. She'd read in her journals that she was trying to turn over a new leaf and start a new life before she went to Paris. Returning from Paris was supposed to be the start of a brand new Holly Carter.

Somewhere along the line she had forgotten about that. She'd become consumed with getting her life back on track but not focused on what she wanted that life to look like.

Moving forward had become more important than moving in a certain direction.

And now there was another mystery to unwrap. The fact that she had admitted being in love with Victoria to Gideon. Had she said anything to Victoria? Did Victoria suspect something? She was an astute woman, able to pick up the smallest of details. Surely, she had seen her second assistant falling in love with her? Was that the reason for Victoria's distance?

Whatever the case, she needed to know for sure or the not knowing was going to tear her apart.

Tonight was the night that Holly would find some answers. She'd spent a lot of time respecting Victoria's boundaries and trying to not bother the publishing titan. But tonight, she wasn't going to allow Victoria to run and hide. Tonight, they were going to talk.

"Holly!" Alexia screeched as she opened the door.

Alexia ran into Holly's arms, and Holly held her tightly. It had been two weeks since she'd seen the girl, and she'd missed her fiercely.

"Hey, it's so good to see you," Holly admitted.

She looked up to see Hugo walking down the stairs. He offered her a small wave, and she smiled back.

"Maybe you should let Holly into the house?" Victoria's voice floated from the kitchen.

Alexia dragged Holly in and closed the door behind them. She started to pull on Holly's jacket to assist her putting it into the closet.

"Mom is making pasta," Alexia said excitedly. "I made the sauce. And then we're going to watch a movie, and th—"

A loud cough came from the kitchen.

"I mean," Alexia corrected, "I'd like to watch a movie if that's okay with you?"

Holly grinned. "That would be great, but only if your mom and your brother join us. I'm here to see everyone, remember?" she said loudly enough for Victoria to hear.

"Cool, they'll join us," Alexia said as if it were already a done deal. Holly presumed it was. Whatever Alexia wanted she generally got. Especially now, she guessed.

She took a deep breath and walked into the kitchen to greet Victoria. As soon as she crossed the threshold, she felt the familiar clenching feeling in her chest. Victoria looked as beautiful as ever.

Her designer clothes were protected by a white apron. She spoke softly to Hugo about his politics homework while she stirred a large saucepan. She hadn't yet noticed Holly in the room. She took the opportunity to enjoy seeing the domestic Victoria most people wouldn't believe existed.

Hugo realised Holly had finally been released from Alexia's clutches and looked at her with a big smile.

"Hey, Holly," he said.

Victoria turned around to follow his gaze. Two sets of piercing green eyes looked at her, and Holly lifted her hand to offer them a cheesy wave.

It was good to be back.

The food was stunning, as Holly had suspected. She didn't believe for one second that Victoria would ever waste her time with something like cooking if she didn't excel at it.

Alexia and Hugo chatted animatedly, making this dinner feel just like the ones she'd enjoyed when she was living at the house.

Unfortunately, it was also exactly the same in that Victoria seemed stilted and withdrawn. Holly tried to draw her into the conversation a couple of times. It worked for a while, but Victoria soon realised what she was doing and retreated back into herself.

Holly had predicted this and had a plan.

"Victoria, I hope you're watching the movie with us?" she asked.

Victoria's fork paused on the way to her mouth. She looked at Holly with slight panic flashing in her eyes.

"I do have some work to do," she said apologetically, not committing herself either way.

"Mom, you promised," Alexia argued.

"Join us," Hugo requested.

Victoria looked at her children and opened her mouth to reply.

"Yes, you must join us," Holly said. "I've been looking forward to seeing you."

Victoria's cheeks started to blush under the pressure. She inclined her head. "Very well, for a little while, at least."

Holly could feel the telltale pressure in her temples. She'd had a few headaches and migraines since she'd been back in New York, and they always started when she was feeling stressed. Picking apart the mystery of Victoria Hastings was certainly stressful.

"Great," Holly said. "What movie are we watching?"

Victoria and Hugo turned towards Alexia, the keeper of the remote control.

"*Toy Story 3*," Alexia replied.

"Do I need to have seen the first two?" Holly asked.

"You'll get the gist," Hugo told her with a roll of his eyes, clearly not excited about the children's movie.

"Hey! They're good movies!" Alexia argued at the slight on her favourite franchise.

"I'm sure they are. I know I must have seen them, even if I don't remember them," Holly interjected to keep the peace.

"Have you remembered anything else?" Alexia probed.

"Alexia," Victoria warned.

"It's okay," Holly said. "I remembered that I don't like cheesecake." She winked at Alexia. She knew the young girl wasn't a fan of the treat either.

"Ick, you should stick to ice cream."

"I will," Holly assured. "And I have a faint memory about skating at Rockefeller Center. I think. There were skaters and really loud music." She was still hazy on that one, but she'd seen a photograph of the rink at Christmas time and it stirred some kind of memory inside her.

"That was for work," Victoria said softly. She straightened and looked a little uncomfortable at the admission. "A photo shoot."

Holly thought about it for a moment. It made sense. It was a memory that had felt stuck to other memories. She remembered the sensation of skating, but she also remembered Victoria being there.

Her headache started to pound, and she winced slightly.

"I have a phone call to make," Victoria announced. "Please start the movie and I will be up as soon as I am able."

She vanished from the dining room. Alexia let out a sigh and pushed her plate to the middle of the table.

"So, how have you guys been?" Holly asked to try to lighten the mood.

"Mom misses you," Alexia said. "She won't admit it, but she does."

"She does," Hugo confirmed.

"I miss her, too," Holly admitted. "I'm going to go and talk to her. I need to fix whatever this is that keeps happening. Are you two okay to start the movie without us?"

Alexia's eyes widened. "What are you going to say?"

"I just want to talk to her. Something is on her mind, and I want her to tell me what it is."

Hugo snorted a laugh. "Good luck."

Holly put her napkin on the table. "Don't worry, I know what I'm doing."

She walked out of the dining room, hoping that Victoria wouldn't call her bluff.

CHAPTER FORTY

Victoria drummed her fingers on the desk. She'd seen the wince on Holly's face at the memory of the Rockefeller shoot. She wished she hadn't said anything. Maybe Holly would have attributed the memory to some delightful day out with friends rather than a terrorising work event.

She narrowed her eyes as she tried to recall the finer details of the day, what she had said, what she had done. She remembered being bitterly cold and frustrated that most of the models were useless on skates.

There was a knock on the door, and she scrambled to pick up her mobile phone and put it to her ear.

"Come in," she called.

Holly walked into the study and closed the door behind her. She walked straight over to the desk and leaned over it, causing Victoria to back up into her chair. Holly snatched the phone and looked at the blank display.

"Thought so," she said smugly. She placed the phone on the desktop, sat in the chair in front of the desk, and looked at Victoria.

Victoria pressed her back into her office chair. Her hand raised, and she started to play with her necklace.

"I was... just finished," Victoria said.

"Of course you were." Holly didn't sound convinced. "We need to talk."

"Do we?"

"We do. I want to know what is going on. Why do you keep hiding out in here?"

Victoria balked. "I am not *hiding out*, I am working."

"No, you're not. I've seen you working, you're focused, you don't hear the knock at the door. And this ... other behaviour... seems to happen around me, so I want to know why."

Victoria wondered if there was a way to escape the room. Her brain wasn't coming up with any useful excuses. She swallowed hard. This was it. They could no longer pretend that Holly didn't recall her terrible behaviour.

"I think you know why," she said.

"No, I don't, that's why I'm here," Holly said plainly. "I don't get it. One minute you're fine, the next you clam up. Or run away."

"I do not run away," Victoria denied.

"You do." Holly folded her arms and sat back in her chair, pinning Victoria with a glare.

Dread was giving way to frustration as Victoria leaned forward.

"If I do, and I'm not saying that I do, but if I do... it's for your benefit. So you don't have to be around me."

Holly frowned. "But... why?"

She slapped her desk. "Because I know you remember! Or you know everything through your journals. I'm sure all twenty-six volumes are dedicated to how... how horrible and spiteful I am!"

Holly's eyes blinked rapidly. A moment later the girl winced and rubbed at her temple.

"And that look," Victoria said as she gestured to Holly. "That... horror at remembering. I saw it after I reminded you about Rockefeller Plaza. You remembered what I said to you. Whatever it was. How I'm expected to remember every single conversation, I don't know."

"Whoa, whoa." Holly held her hands up. "I don't remember. And this look, this is a headache starting. Which, by the way, you are causing because you stress me out."

Victoria felt the wind leave her sails. "You... don't remember?"

"No. If I'd had memories, then I would have told you. Why do you..." Holly's eyes widened. "Oh my god, is that what all of this has been about? Have you been worried that I've remembered working with you? And you... you've been taking yourself out of the situation. For me?"

Victoria's nose flared. She felt like she was being mocked. "But your journals..."

"My journals told me a lot about my life," Holly admitted. "And, yes, they did say that you were a royal bitch most of the time. But I don't care. Did you worry that I... what? That I hated you?"

"You will hate me," Victoria said with dead seriousness. "It will come."

"No, it won't," Holly replied.

"It will. You may not remember now, but one day you will. And that is why I pulled away. For your sake. Because I knew that one day you would remember how terrible I was to you, and it would break us apart."

"Assuming the worst," Holly closed her eyes and mumbled to herself.

"What?" Victoria asked.

"Nothing. I'm just realising how dumb I've been." Holly opened her eyes and looked at Victoria. "Nothing could make me hate you."

Victoria chuckled. "I wish I could believe that. But I remember what I was like, even if you don't."

Holly abruptly stood up and walked to the door. "Don't move," she commanded before leaving the room.

Victoria stared after her in shock. She couldn't believe the girl was being so forward. Things had changed. She let out a breath that had become trapped in her lungs. The breath she felt she had been holding since the first time she worried about Holly's memories returning.

She didn't understand. Holly said her journals were accurate if the royal bitch comment was anything to go by. And yet Holly hadn't immediately run away.

Holly burst back into the room with her bag and closed the door behind her. She opened her bag and pulled out a journal.

Victoria rolled her eyes. She didn't need this. She didn't need to hear the contents of her former second assistant's diary. She didn't want to hear how she had made Holly cry or despair.

Holly sat down and opened the journal. She flipped through a few pages before she found what she was looking for.

"'She wasn't in the office today'," she read aloud.

"'Louise was relieved, but I was depressed. A day without Victoria feels like a wasted day'."

Victoria gasped. She tensed; waiting for the other shoe to drop.

"'I'm hoping when she returns that it will be a late night to catch up. I'll volunteer, of course. Louise thinks I'm sucking up, aiming for a promotion before her. But the idea of promotion terrifies me. Because if I am promoted, I'll move to another department. And I don't want that, I want to be here'."

Holly flipped over a few pages before stopping again and reading further.

"'She sent me on three pointless errands today. I don't mind. I achieved everything she wanted, no matter how impossible she thought it might be. Seeing her surprise when I return with what she needs is captivating. I'm sure she doesn't think so. I love being the one who impresses her'."

Victoria shook her head. Surely, she was reading the wrong meaning into Holly's text.

Holly turned a few more pages. Her cheeks were starting to redden.

"'She's beautiful today. I think she's caught me staring a couple of times. Part of me wishes she would… wishes she would realise that I'm madly in l-love with her'," Holly stammered momentarily. She sat up straighter and continued. "'Then at least this torture would be over. Most likely she'd relocate me to another *Arrival* office altogether. But in my dreams, she'd smile softly as I have seen her do when she is on the phone with her children'."

The room started to spin. Victoria finally connected the

dots and realised what she had done. Suddenly the throwaway comment from over a year ago came back and hit her so hard she thought she might black out.

She jumped to her feet. "You should leave," she told Holly.

Holly looked up at her, her face ashen, tears forming in her eyes.

"You've done nothing wrong," Victoria amended. "But you really ought to leave."

"I just wanted to tell you how I felt," Holly said. "I wanted to explain to you that I could never hate you. I loved you, even then. I don't expect anything from you. We can pretend it never happened, I just... needed you to know that I could never hate you. There's nothing that you could do to make me hate you."

Victoria shook her head. "There is, you just don't recall it yet."

Holly dropped her journal heavily onto Victoria's desk and stood up as well.

"Then tell me! Stop holding this knowledge over me. It's not fair, Victoria. Whatever it is that you know, or think you know, then tell me. I can't keep going on like this."

"It's my fault you walked away!" Victoria shouted back.

Holly backed up a step, never having heard her raise her voice.

"I am the reason all of this happened." Victoria walked over to the study door and held it open. "Without me, you wouldn't have memory loss, you wouldn't have lost an entire *year* of your life."

Holly walked over to the door. She slammed it closed

and leaned her arm on the solid wood, her face was centimetres from Victoria's.

"No more secrets, tell me," Holly demanded.

Victoria cleared her throat softly.

"I… I didn't know then," she clarified before she told her tale. "I didn't know you had feelings for me—"

"Loved you," Holly corrected.

She swallowed. Holly was so close to her. She could smell her scent. This would probably be the last time that Holly would look at her positively. She tried to take it all in so she would remember the moment.

"We'd been at an afternoon drinks reception," Victoria explained. "In the car, you suggested… that you cared for me. Just cared, nothing more. Of course, I had no idea of the strength of your feelings. And I thought you were drunk. I…" She turned her head away, not wanting to see Holly's face. "I told you that you were being ridiculous. And I asked why you thought I should even acknowledge your existence, I told you that you were nothing to me. Just a second assistant, like hundreds of girls before you."

Victoria closed her eyes. She wondered if Holly was a violent person. She wouldn't blame Holly if she struck her.

"I didn't know how deep your feelings ran. I can see now that that conversation must have broken your heart. And set in motion the whole chain of events."

CHAPTER FORTY-ONE

Holly took a step back from Victoria. Her hands trembled as she pressed a palm to her racing heart. Victoria was probably right; the rejection of her feelings had probably sent her running away. But that was irrelevant now.

Victoria was pressed against the study door, her head turned to the side and her eyes tightly closed. She couldn't imagine the pressure Victoria had been under. Keeping that last conversation bottled up must have been torture, even if she hadn't understood the magnitude of her actions until this moment.

Not to mention living in fear that, at any moment, Holly could be struck with the memories of her behaviour.

She reached out a shaky hand and took Victoria's.

Victoria's eyes flew open, and she inhaled nervously.

Holly gently tugged on her hand, pulled her away from the door, and gestured for her to sit on the sofa. Victoria did what she was told. She sat primly on the edge of her seat, looking like she was waiting for the world to end.

Holly sat on the coffee table in front of Victoria. Their knees almost touched.

"I have never, and will never, blame you for what happened. Even now," Holly said very clearly. "Whatever you might have said, I made the choice to walk away. I fell in love with you, I acted on it, and I must have known what might have happened. I decided to leave you, and I got into an accident. You didn't push me in front of a bus," she paused before joking, "did you?"

Victoria let out a hesitant laugh. "No, no, I can assure you that I didn't."

"I'm sorry that you've been living with this guilt," Holly said.

"I'm fine—"

"No, you're not." Holly leaned forward and wiped the escaped tear that ran down Victoria's cheek. "You can't keep things bottled up like that."

"I had no idea that you felt—"

"Feel," Holly corrected. She watched Victoria swallow.

"Holly… I'm flattered. But I'm positive it's not love that you feel," Victoria spoke softly, refusing to make eye contact. "It's probably nothing more than hero worship. Or Stockholm syndrome." She chuckled.

"I thought so, too," Holly admitted. "But it isn't. And being here with you proved to me that it is love."

"I-I'm completely wrong for you," Victoria said hastily. "I'm over twenty years your senior. I have two children. I'm divorced, impossible to live with, married to my job."

Holly's heart froze for a split second before it started pounding in her chest. Her eyes widened, and her eyebrows rose.

"You're… telling me why you are wrong for me," Holly whispered.

"Of course I'm wrong for you," Victoria replied.

"But you're not telling me that you don't feel the same way."

All the colour drained from Victoria's face at once. It might have been comical if it wasn't so serious.

"I don't care about your age," Holly explained. "I love your children, and they like me. Alexia thinks I'm way cool, don't forget. So what if you're divorced? What was the next one? Oh, yeah, impossible to live with. I've lived with you, and I didn't find it impossible. I loved it. And I don't mean the luxurious guestroom. I mean the time I shared with you, which wasn't much because you kept running away. But I always wanted more, even before I knew what I felt for you."

"Y-you are confusing love and gratitude. Because I brought you home."

Holly stood up and pressed Victoria back into the sofa. She straddled her, taking her face in her hands and pressing the lightest of kisses to her lips.

Victoria's arms wrapped around her back. She stared up at Holly with astonishment.

"Does this feel like gratitude?" Holly asked.

She slowly dipped down to kiss her again. Unhurriedly, to give Victoria the time to come to her senses and push her away. Just in case Holly had completely misread the situation.

But Victoria reached up and pulled her in close. Their lips met and Holly let out a gasp. She couldn't believe her luck. She was straddling Victoria Hastings, kissing her and being held tightly by her. It was her dreams come true.

"Mom!"

Holly jumped backwards, tripped over the coffee table, and wobbled for a few moments before miraculously righting herself.

"Impressive," Victoria said. "Though she is two floors away. She just has extraordinary lungs."

Holly's heart was pounding. Victoria got up and opened the study door.

"Yes, darling?"

"Hurry up, we want to see Holly, too," Alexia shouted from the upstairs of the house.

"We'll be there shortly," Victoria promised. She closed the door and faced Holly.

Holly was out of clever things to say. She felt exhausted. The last couple of hours had been an emotional rollercoaster, and her headache wasn't giving up. But Victoria didn't look mad. In fact, she was smiling.

"Maybe we should go to dinner. Together. Alone," Victoria suggested. "Soon."

Holly's eyes widened. "I'd like that. Tomorrow?" she suggested. She didn't want too much time to pass.

"Tomorrow," Victoria agreed. "I can spend some more time explaining how wrong I am for you." A smile curled at her lips.

"Good, that gives me the chance to tell you how wrong you are and how right we are together." Holly grinned. "Can I kiss you again?"

"I don't know, can you?"

Holly rolled her eyes at the semantics. She walked across the room, her arms outstretched. She was relieved and ecstatic when Victoria met her halfway. They fell into each other's arms. They fit together perfectly.

Holly didn't bother with a chaste, sweet kiss this time. This time, she put all of her feelings into it. She moved her lips softly but firmly over Victoria's, demonstrating how she felt. Victoria moaned into her mouth.

Having zero memories of any previous romantic encounters made the whole situation even more surreal for Holly. She'd dreamed about this moment. Both before and after her accident, by all accounts. And now she was lip-locked with Victoria. Literally the woman of her dreams.

Soft lips, gently roaming hands, the scent of expensive perfume. Everything magnified and yet so fleeting. She knew it would be over soon. But, for now, she wanted to take everything in, memorise every tiny detail.

Victoria seemed to be out of air, so Holly softly ended the kiss.

They stared at one another in silence for a moment, wide smiles gracing both their faces.

"We should join the kids," Holly suggested.

"We should. But I don't think I'm going to be able to keep this ridiculous grin from my face," Victoria admitted. "I should probably warn you that Hugo suspects my feelings for you."

"Alexia knows I have feelings for you," Holly confessed. "I didn't tell her, she guessed."

Victoria's eyebrows raised. "So… that certainly makes things easier."

"It does." Holly took her hand. "Sit next to me for the movie?"

Victoria blushed as she looked at their connected hands. "Try to stop me."

CHAPTER FORTY-TWO

Victoria really couldn't understand Alexia's obsession with the *Toy Story* movies. That said, she was grateful that they were thoroughly dull so she could spend her time exchanging meaningful glances with Holly.

She wanted nothing more than to return to the study and discuss what they were doing. What the future held and whether or not she was kidding herself for thinking that any kind of a relationship with Holly might work. She also wanted to kiss the girl again. It had been a great number of months since she last shared a romantic kiss with someone, and she wasn't even slightly satisfied.

Of course the kiss had been magnificent. More than she could ever have expected, but now she found herself wanting more. She felt like a teenager all over again.

The movie paused.

She looked up and frowned before seeing Hugo with the remote in his hand, a cheeky grin on his face.

"Okay, you two, what's going on?" he asked. He pointed to the two of them with the remote control.

"What do you mean?" she replied. She sat up a little straighter and attempted to look nonchalant.

"We're going on a date tomorrow," Holly announced.

Victoria stared at the side of her head, wondering where the girl got her courage from.

"Cool," Hugo said. He looked at her. "Way to go, Mom."

She felt her cheeks warm.

"*Fi*-nally," Alexia said. "I was getting old waiting for you two to figure it out."

Holly laughed and launched a tickle attack on Alexia. The two of them fell from the sofa to the floor of the living room and started to roll around as they attacked one another.

The screeches and giggles made Victoria laugh. She caught Hugo's eye, and he smiled at her. She smiled back before indicating the pair on the ground with a tilt of her head. He nodded in agreement.

They both pounced, Hugo grabbing and tickling Alexia and Victoria trying to do the same with Holly. Sadly, Holly was stronger and easily turned the situation around.

In a matter of seconds, Victoria was on her back, and all three of them were tickling her. She laughed loudly, pleading them to stop but secretly loving every moment of it. Maybe she was forty-seven, but right then she felt no older than Alexia.

"Mercy, mercy!" she eventually cried when breathing was becoming a struggle. Hugo and Holly stopped immediately, but Alexia continued on. She grabbed Alexia and pulled her into a tight cuddle to stop her little fingers from finding her ribs.

"I'm proud of you, Mom," Alexia whispered, her face centimetres away.

"Thank you, darling."

Alexia wiggled out of her grip and stood up. She smoothed her hair out and looked at Holly, who was resting on the sofa.

"Does this mean you'll move back in with us now?" Alexia asked.

Holly shook her head. "No, sorry, Alexia."

Victoria felt her heart drop. She had hoped that Holly might agree to move back. She'd missed her terribly. And moving into the guestroom wasn't really moving in together in her eyes.

"But why?" Alexia whined.

Yes, why? Victoria thought.

"Because I need my independence," Holly said. "I need some time and space in my own place, so I can miss you guys all the more. And so I have the best possible chance of making this work with your mom. I want us to be equals. As equal as we can be, anyway."

Victoria got up from the floor and pulled Alexia to her.

"It will be for the best, darling. Don't worry, Holly will visit us very often." She looked meaningfully at Holly.

"I will," Holly promised as their eyes met.

Victoria felt a buzz of excitement run through her body. She didn't know what would happen next, but she knew she was going to make an effort to be more transparent. Assumptions and gloomy predictions had nearly torn her and Holly apart. She wasn't going to let that happen again.

They all sat in their respective seats again, and Hugo started up the movie.

She felt Holly's arm wrap around her shoulder, and she leaned into the one-armed hug. She listened to the steady rhythm of Holly's heartbeat and looked at her two children.

This was something she could get used to. Something she *would* get used to, she promised herself.

She turned to Holly and pressed a quick kiss to her cheek. Then she rested her head on Holly's chest and let out a satisfied sigh.

CHAPTER FORTY-THREE

Holly dropped her suitcase onto the bench at the end of the bed with a grunt. Each time she moved, the case got a little heavier. She supposed that was a good sign.

She slid the zipper around the case and flipped the lid open.

"Would you like any help?"

She turned and saw a very smug-looking Victoria in the doorway.

"No, thank you. You'll only critique my clothes." Holly returned to what she was doing.

"I'm getting better at that," Victoria sought praise.

"You are," Holly confessed. "I'm fine to unpack by myself, but I'd like the company though."

Victoria entered the guestroom and sat in the armchair by the window.

"Amazing that my house was suddenly bought by some anonymous developer," Holly mused.

Victoria turned to look out of the window. "Not surprising, it was practically falling down. I'm sure a new property there would turn a good profit. For whoever purchased it."

Holly knew that Victoria had bought the property. It was such a *Victoria* way to ask her to move in. She was secretly pleased, being back under the Hastings roof was a dream. But she wouldn't let Victoria off the hook too easily.

"Thank goodness your guestroom was still available," Holly said.

Victoria turned to look at her seriously. "You'll always have a place here, no matter what happens."

She knew Victoria meant it, too.

"I appreciate that."

Holly picked up a stack of clothes and piled them into the chest of drawers, ignoring Victoria's sigh. She didn't know if that was because Holly was bunching up clothes and shoving them into a drawer, or because of the low-quality clothing she preferred over the designer couture that Victoria bought her.

Of course, Victoria was doing remarkably well in other ways at accepting that Holly wanted to be independent in many things.

"What time is the gala tonight?" Holly asked.

"Eight. I intend to arrive at nine."

"And you're sure you want to go together?"

Victoria chuckled. "Of course. We've been seen out several times. Tongues are already wagging, we may as well confirm suspicions. As long as you're sure?"

Victoria's doubts crept up every now and then, and Holly was always quick to quash them. She dropped a handful of socks back into the suitcase and walked over to the armchair where she knelt in front of Victoria and looked up at her.

"Am I sure that I want to be seen with and linked to the most beautiful woman in New York?" Holly asked with a grin.

Victoria blushed and looked away. "Stop," she muttered, but it was obvious she enjoyed the compliment.

Holly stood up and pressed a soft kiss to Victoria's cheek before returning to her unpacking. She'd need to hurry if she was going to unpack, eat, and get herself ready for a gala.

"You know what they'll say?" Victoria attempted to sound disinterested, but it didn't fool Holly.

"That I'm a gold digger?" Holly asked.

"That I'm a cradle robber," Victoria said.

"I don't care what they say," Holly confessed. "I just pity anyone who doesn't feel as happy as I feel every day."

It was true. She was happy every day. Overwhelmingly so. They'd been dating for just over two months. They'd quickly undone the power of attorney to provide Holly with the autonomy that she desperately sought. As far as she was concerned, Victoria still owned her heart.

Victoria had used her contacts to provide Holly with the opportunity to write for a couple of large lifestyle websites. She still worked part-time as a receptionist, but the side income was steadily growing, and she knew that before long she'd be able to work from home and focus on her writing.

While Victoria had used her network, Holly knew that she had only been accepted based on her skills. Most significantly, Victoria had understood how important that was to

Holly. It would have been easy to just click into Victoria's family and live a life of luxury without having to lift a finger. But Holly would have been miserable. She had to find her own success.

She realised that she had been caught in her own little dream world for a while, and Victoria had yet to speak. She looked up and caught the older woman staring at her with a slack jaw.

"What?" Holly asked.

"I… I'm just surprised to hear you say that. I feel the same way," she admitted.

"I know. I can read you like a book." Holly winked.

Victoria rolled her eyes. "Hardly."

Nearly, Holly thought. She'd gotten very good at reading Victoria over recent weeks.

"How much will the house cost to renovate?" Holly asked.

"We're not renovating, we're tearing it down and—" Victoria's eyes widened and she stopped her mouth immediately.

"I knew it!" Holly jumped for glee at being able to trick her. "I knew it was you. I told you that my room was cold, that I saw *one* cockroach in the *yard*, and suddenly the landlord has an offer he can't refuse and gives us all one-week notice. I knew it was you."

"You were living in third-world conditions," Victoria defended her actions. "I couldn't, in good conscience, allow you to carry on your recovery there."

"You know I'm all but recovered, right? My physio is next to nothing, it's basically an exercise class these days. And my memory, well, nothing's changing there."

"How do you feel about that?" Victoria asked.

"About my memories not returning?"

Victoria nodded.

Holly shrugged. "It's fine. If I remember things, then that's great, but if I don't, that's fine, too. I'm more invested in the new memories that I have now. And my journals have given me loads of information on things that happened before."

She knew that Victoria still worried about Holly's memories returning and Holly running for the hills. Holly did everything she could to reassure Victoria that would never happen.

It was remarkable how sensitive Victoria was. Holly would never have guessed that beneath the cool exterior lived a very insecure woman. But she loved it. It gave her the opportunity to constantly offer love and support, and Victoria lapped it up.

"Knock knock." Gideon's voice floated down the stairs from the main hallway. "Can I come down? Are you all decent?"

Victoria rolled her eyes and shook her head. Gideon had been teasing them about their relationship since the moment Holly accidentally let it slip.

Holly chuckled. "Come on down," she called back.

He entered the guestroom and looked at them both with a cocky grin.

"Moving in together already, so sweet," he drawled. "Though you are taking the separate bedrooms thing to a whole new level."

Holly noticed the light tint of a blush on Victoria's cheeks.

"I'm sure I won't be down here for long," Holly said. "When you've found someone you want to be with, it's hard to stay away. Even if you feel you should for the sake of respectability."

Victoria looked mightily pleased with herself. She raised her chin and looked towards the window. "To hell with respectability," she murmured.

Gideon looked as surprised as Holly felt, but he gathered himself together quickly enough.

"Hear, hear," he said. He turned to Holly. "Now, what are you wearing for the gala? The Valentino, surely?"

Although he was facing Holly, it was obvious that the question was directed to Victoria.

"Of course," she said. "She'll be the talk of the town."

"She will," Gideon agreed. "You both will."

"I've been trying to convince her to stay home," Victoria said. "To save herself."

Holly chuckled. She walked over to the armchair where Victoria sat like a queen and deposited herself in her lap. She wrapped her arms around Victoria's shoulders.

"And I've been trying to tell her that it's all worth it and that I've never been happier."

"One day, I'll convince you how wrong I am for you," Victoria joked.

"Never," Holly said adamantly. "You're the person who found me when I had nothing, you breathed life back into me. And then I found out that I'd been in love with you before I even knew who you were. I'm never letting you go."

"Good, because listening to you both complaining about each other was such a dreary pity party," Gideon said.

Holly looked at Victoria and raised her eyebrow. "Shall I?"

"Yes, do."

Holly reached down, pulled her Converse Low Top off her foot, and threw it at him.

It just missed him as he rushed out into the hallway.

"I'll be upstairs when you can behave yourselves," he said between fits of laughter.

Holly giggled. She turned to Victoria. "I don't think I can behave myself," she said seriously.

"Me neither," Victoria admitted as she reached up for a kiss.

THE STORY CONTINUES...

If you enjoyed Bring Holly Home then you'll love the free short story, Holly Hollydays.

Request your free copy at my website now

http://aeradley.com/holly-hollydays

ALSO BY AMANDA RADLEY

KEEP HOLLY CLOSE

Former personal assistant Holly Carter is settling into her new life as a mother, a journalist, and partner of magazine editor —and former boss—Victoria Hastings.

The arrival of an anonymous email threatens to split the happy couple up. They have to work together but will they be able to overcome both Holly's amnesia and Victoria's reserved demeanour to find the perpetrator?

PATREON

I adore publishing. There's a wonderful thrill that comes from crafting a manuscript and then releasing it to the world. Especially when you are writing woman loving woman characters. I'm blessed to receive messages from readers all over the world who are thrilled to discover characters and scenarios that resemble their lives.

Books are entertaining escapism, but they are also reinforcement that we are not alone in our struggles. I'm passionate about writing books that people can identify with. Books that are accessible to all and show that love—and acceptance—can be found no matter who you are.

I've been lucky enough to have published books that have been best-sellers and even some award-winners. While I'm still quite a new author, I have plans to write many, many more novels. However, writing, editing, and marketing books take up a lot of time… and writing full-time is a treadmill-like existence, especially in a very small niche market like mine.

Don't get me wrong, I feel very grateful and lucky to be

able to live the life I do. But being a full-time author in a small market means never being able to stop and work on developing my writing style, it means rarely having the time or budget to properly market my books, it means immediately picking up the next project the moment the previous has finished.

This is why I have set up a Patreon account. With Patreon, you can donate a small amount each month to enable me to hop off of my treadmill for a while in order to reach my goals. Goals such as exploring better marketing options, developing my writing craft, and investigating writing articles and screenplays.

My Patreon page is a place for exclusive first looks at new works, insight into upcoming projects, Q&A sessions, as well as special gifts and dedications. I'm also pleased to give all of my Patreon subscribers access to **exclusive short stories** which have been written just for patrons. There are tiers to suit all budgets.

My readers are some of the kindest and most supportive people I have met, and I appreciate every book borrow or purchase. With the added support of Patreon, I hope to be able to develop my writing career in order to become a better author as well as level up my marketing strategy to help my books to reach a wider audience.

https://www.patreon.com/aeradley

REVIEWS

I sincerely hope you enjoyed reading this book.

If you did, I would greatly appreciate a short review on your favourite book website.

Reviews are crucial for any author, and even just a line or two can make a huge difference.

ABOUT THE AUTHOR

Amanda Radley had no desire to be a writer but accidentally became an award-winning, bestselling author.

She gave up a marketing career in order to make stuff up for a living instead. She claims the similarities are startling.

She describes herself as a Wife. Traveller. Tea Drinker. Biscuit Eater. Animal Lover. Master Pragmatist. Procrastinator. Theme Park Fan.

Connect with Amanda
www.amandaradley.com

ALSO BY AMANDA RADLEY

FITTING IN

2020 Amazon Kindle Storyteller Finalist

Starting a new job is hard. Especially if you're the boss's daughter

Heather Bailey has been in charge of Silver Arches, the prestigious London shopping centre, for several years. Financial turmoil brings a new investor to secure the future and Heather finds herself playing office politics with the notoriously difficult entrepreneur Leo Flynn. Walking a fine line between standing her ground and being willing to accept change, Heather has her work cut out for her.

When Leo demands that his daughter is found a job at Silver Arches; things become even harder.

Scarlett Flynn has never fit in. Not in the army, not in her father's firm, not even in her own family. So starting work at Silver Arches won't be any different, will it?

A heartwarming exploration of the art of fitting in.

ALSO BY AMANDA RADLEY

GOING UP

2020 Selfies Finalist

A ruthless executive. A destitute woman. Both on the way up.

Selina Hale is on her way to the top. She's been working towards a boardroom position on the thirteenth floor for her entire career. And no one is going to get in her way. Not her clueless boss, her soon to be ex-wife, and most certainly not the homeless person who has moved into the car park at work.

Kate Morgan fell through the cracks in a broken support system and found herself destitute. Determined and strong-willed, she's not about to accept help from a mean business woman who can't even remember the names of her own nephews.

As their lives continue to intertwine, they have no choice but to work together and follow each other on their journey up.

ALSO BY AMANDA RADLEY

SECOND CHANCES

Bad childhood memories start to resurface when Hannah Hall's daughter Rosie begins school. To make matters more complicated, Hannah has been steadfastly ignoring the obvious truth that Rosie is intellectually gifted and wise beyond her years.

In the crumbling old school she meets Rosie's new teacher Alice Spencer who has moved from the city to teach in the small coastal town of Fairlight.

Alice immediately sees Rosie's potential and embarks on developing an educational curriculum to suit Rosie's needs, to Hannah's dismay.

Teacher and mother clash over what's best for young Rosie.

Will they be able to compromise? Will Hannah finally open up to someone about her own damaged upbringing?

And will they be able to ignore the sparks that fly whenever they are in the same room?

Copyright © 2018 Amanda Radley

All rights reserved. No part of this book may be reproduced in any form on by an electronic or mechanical means, including information storage and retrieval systems, without permission in writing from the publisher, except by a reviewer who may quote brief passages in a review.

This is a work of fiction. Names, characters, places, and incidents either are the product of the author's imagination or are used fictitiously. Any resemblance to actual persons, living or dead, events, or locales is entirely coincidental.

Printed in Great Britain
by Amazon